Formen

To

From the
Weaver of the Web

FLASHFLOOD . . .

Electricity had been turned off. There was no need for it. No one lived here now. The cold wind from the open door blew across the bare floorboards. It followed Taylor into the house like a storm spirit or a wandering ghost.

Her grandmother's bedroom was on the second floor, at the far end of the hallway. She wished she'd brought a flashlight. The hall seemed longer and darker than she remembered, full of places where something could hide. Someone.

What if her grandmother's ghost was in this house? What if she saw a pale, shadowy figure moving toward her? What should she do? Run?

But it wasn't her grandmother she feared so much. What scared her were other things . . . things her grandmother had protected her from when she was around, but maybe couldn't protect her from now. It was the unknown that made Taylor feel strange and a little afraid to be alone in the silence of this house.

She turned the knob of Grandma Jane's bedroom door and stepped inside.

In that bed, Taylor thought. The idea almost stopped her. Weren't ghosts supposed to stay in places where they'd died? This place? This room?

The Spider's Child

Volume 3
Flashflood

Jessica Pierce

Z·FAVE
KENSINGTON PUBLISHING CORP.

To the memory of my mother,
Juanette Hobbs Fields, who told
this bedtime story so long ago.

Chapter One

It was nearly closing when the child entered Broadmore's Used Books and Antiquities. Light from the storefront window was cast with the purple and pink of the outside sky. Nearly dusk. Twilight, a magical time when dreams and reality are suspended and blend, slipping into each other as easily as day slips into night.

The store was like a place in a dream. Ten-year-old Taylor McKenzie moved along its narrow aisles, letting the flat of her fingers trail over the smooth planes of tables, standing bookshelves, and elaborately carved chairs. This was more than a bookstore. She'd felt that certainty from the moment she'd stepped inside. The front door was the entrance to an enchanted world. Pieces of dreams were all around her.

"I need a book," said Taylor in a voice she tried to keep from shaking, "a very special book."

"Who sent you?" asked Mr. Ambrose, the proprietor.

Taylor drew up her courage and spoke what she felt was the answer to his question. "My grandmother told me this was the place to find your dreams . . . if you've lost them."

It would be night soon. She had come out deliberately at twilight, because that was a magical time, but now she realized she'd have to walk home alone in the dark. She was afraid of the dark. Awareness of that quickened her search to find the book. She had to hurry. Night wouldn't wait.

"Look on the shelves," said Mr. Ambrose. "The book will find you."

She thought it strange, how he'd said that. The book would find *her?* Didn't he mean it the other way around? It was nearly too dark in the shop to see the titles along the spines of the books. She wished he would turn on a light, but didn't see one anywhere. Not a bulb, not a lamp, nothing.

The store was full of interesting things. Standing near the entrance was a knight's suit of armor, complete with helmet and visor. It stood facing the door, as if guarding the property. She cautiously passed the standing knight, tempted to lift the rim of his helmet visor and peek inside, but afraid of what she might see.

Hanging from the ceiling was a large, round spiderweb. On closer inspection, Taylor realized that the web was woven string tied to a wooden hoop. A turquoise bead was strung near the web's center, and a single feather hung down from the top of the hoop and over the face of the web.

A small tag dangled from the bottom of the hoop. Taylor reached for it and read: *Dreamcatcher, of Native American design. It is hung over a sleeping child to catch bad dreams in the web and keep them from the sleeper. A small opening at the web's center allows good dreams to flow through to the child.*

Taylor hadn't seen an opening in the web. She looked again. *There* was an opening, hidden beneath the feather. The wonderful image stayed with her, a lacy spiderweb strung with turquoise beads like planets stretching across the night sky, and an opening where goodness flowed through to dreamers. The image of the feather lingered, too, like a feathery cloud hiding the opening.

So many things of wonder were in the store, but she had to hurry.

Along one aisle, a lingering amber glow from the window filtered over one row of a standing oak bookcase. Attracted by the light, she drew nearer. The many volumes along the shelf were heavy and thick, too full of words for the dream she wanted.

And then it found her, just as Mr. Ambrose had said it would. She felt the book's presence before she saw it, knew it had waited only for her. The gold lettering along the spine read: *The Spider's Child.* For a moment, she stared at it in awed silence, knowing this was the one. It wasn't clear how she knew it, but she did.

The book was old, its edges worn and frayed. Taylor lifted it from the shelf, separating the aged leather volume from the others by the thin border of her hand. The amber glow from the fading sunlight bathed the book's crackling pages in a comforting bloom of warmth.

Carefully, she turned each page, until she came to one with a handwritten verse. Beside an intricately drawn pen-and-ink spiderweb, and another title, *Flashflood,* were these lines:

> *You are her young, the Spider's Child.*
> *Clutched in her Web, so tender and mild.*
> *Enter this book, and she'll take you there.*
> *Caught in the threads of the Spider's lair.*

Who was the Spider? What kind of book was this? she wondered. *Had it really picked me?*

Daring with all her heart, Taylor turned the page. There was another poem, this one chilling her as she read it:

> *Any and all assorted fear,*
> *turn the page,*
> *you will find it here.*

Beside this was the smooth black ink of an inscription, flowing like silk over the rough texture of the page. *To Taylor,* the dedication read. *From the Weaver of the Web.*

This *was* the one; she knew it. The book was dedicated to her. How could it be meant for anyone else? In the pages of this book, she would try to find her dream.

"Is it very much?" she asked, holding the book toward Mr. Ambrose, noticing for the first time how still he was behind his desk. He hadn't moved from it since she'd entered the store.

His hair and mustache were whiter than the pages of the book. For an instant, she imagined him in clothes far different from the business suit he wore . . . in a costume of a flowing white woolen robe, hooded. His hair would be longer and loose about his shoulders, and his eyes . . . Even in the near dark, Taylor could see the bright blue of his eyes.

"I will ask only one thing of you for the loan of this book," said Mr. Ambrose. "That you return with it to Broadmore's when you have found your dream."

Taylor nodded. There was something of the future in this promise. It scared her a little. What if something happened and she couldn't return it? What if—

"I knew your grandmother," said Mr. Ambrose. "I'm sorry for her death. I know how much you miss her."

Taylor felt the quick sting of tears threaten her eyes. It surprised and shocked her that this stranger recognized the deep scar of pain she'd carried since the recent death of her grandmother. She looked away, trying to hide the tears that spilled from her eyes and down her cheeks.

"I have to go home," she said.

Home wasn't a place she wanted to be, not since . . .

"Don't be afraid of finding your way into the story," said Mr. Ambrose. "A novel is a waking dream, and this one is for you."

She held the book tightly as she left the store, knowing Mr. Ambrose's eyes were watching her as she passed the glass storefront window. *What does he see in me?* she wondered. *What does he know that I don't know?*

A flash of lightning scored the darkening sky. Seconds later, a clap of thunder broke overhead. Startled, she felt the coming storm as if she were a part of it, as if the lightning, thunder, and the raging rain were inside her mind.

Racing before the approaching storm, Taylor hurried home.

Mr. Ambrose felt the storm coming, too. Dark did not frighten him. He was a fragment of light, and felt no terror of the dark. Held in the dark of the sky were fiery stars, the world of Earth, and planets like gleaming jewels strung across the sky.

When the child had gone, Mr. Ambrose walked to

the place where the Dreamcatcher hung from the ceiling. *Yes,* he thought, *this is for her.* Hadn't she come into the shop searching for a dream she'd lost?

Each item in Broadmore's Used Books and Antiquities belonged to someone. Each book and each antique or curiosity was intended for one person, and one person only. Taylor McKenzie didn't know it yet, but the Dreamcatcher belonged to her.

Mr. Ambrose knew the weaving of her Web, the fearful edges where it seemed she was cast alone. If she could only find her way to the center, to where the good dreams flowed . . .

In the dark of the coming storm, he waited.

Chapter Two

Fear walked beside her as the overhead sky changed from burnished purple to silvered black, and bolts of lightning sheared through the dark like hurled spears. Thunder broke around her, shattering the silence of the night.

Taylor feared the dark, and what lay hidden within it. Now, she walked home as quickly as she dared, holding the book against her like a shield. Who would protect her now that Grandma Jane was gone?

The thought made the hurt of losing her grandmother fresh again. It stabbed through her like the lightning spears. The hurt shuddered through her mind and heart, like the thunder overhead.

Instead of pushing these thoughts away, she tried to pull the pain closer, holding onto it. This was all she had left of her grandmother. Maybe, she thought, if she'd known Grandma Jane was sick, she might have been prepared for what happened, might have been ready to lose her. But it had happened so quickly.

Her heart, the doctors had said. She'd died in her sleep.

Now, Taylor's sleep was filled with frightening dreams. She feared the death that had come so quickly to her grandmother and had taken her without any warning. Without a chance for Taylor to say goodbye.

The first drops of rain began to fall. She tucked the book beneath her green sweater to keep it dry. The drops were hard, like stinging points of a needle. She lowered her head, trying to protect her eyes and face. In seconds, heavy rain beat down on her exposed neck and trickled in cold rivulets under the sweater's neck band, and down her back.

She was cold, wearing only the green sweater, faded blue jeans, thick white socks, and tennis shoes. Her feet were icy from the puddles she'd stepped into at street corners; the water had soaked through the porous canvas of the shoes. Her straight brown hair, parted on one side, usually fell in a tapered line to just below her ears. Except now, it hung in straggly cords like a mop dripping into her eyes. Cold and wet, she ran toward home, as if something hidden in the night were chasing her.

Home was not a place she liked to be. It wasn't a bad place, not cruel or scary. But it was empty. Her father lived with her at home. To Taylor, he seemed a stranger.

Her mother had died when Taylor was a baby. A car accident had taken her mother's life in an instant, without warning. After that, Taylor had spent a lot of time with Grandma Jane, her mother's mother.

Nearly every day, especially when she was little, her father had brought her to Grandma Jane's tall wooden house. She stayed with her grandmother while her father worked. Her father didn't talk to Taylor much, and so it was a relief to come into Grandma Jane's house, where words flowed easily, and the sounds of singing and laughter echoed in the halls.

Now, the halls were quiet. Grandma Jane was gone. Like Taylor's mother, without warning.

In the distance, she saw lights in the windows of the house she shared with her father, the image distorted by the rain, the square panes of light wavering. Lights meant her father was home.

Would he be worried? she wondered. *No, he doesn't care.*

Seeing the lights of home, she walked more slowly. The lonely house with its quiet rooms had never made her feel welcome.

"I was worried about you."

Her father, John McKenzie, met Taylor at the

door, a look of concern narrowing his eyes and pulling his forehead into deep creases between his brows. "Now that your grandmother's gone, you've got to be more responsible," he said. "I have to be able to depend on you."

"I'm sorry." It was all she could think to say.

"You wouldn't believe all the things I've been imagining, waiting here for you. This storm, the lightning, I thought you might have been hit by a car . . . like your mother."

That hurt. Why did he have to compare them? She wasn't her mother. Why did he have to remind her that both her mother and her grandmother were gone? She felt the storm raining inside her again, like hidden tears.

"I try to do my best for you," he said. "I want us to be a family, the two of us, only I'm not sure how to make it happen. Your grandmother kept us together, kept everything in place. Now, I . . ."

She wanted to scream at him. *Stop it!* She didn't want to hear about her grandmother or her mother, or how they were all that was left, the two of them. She couldn't stand to think that way. Talking about the losses was like being forced to see the pieces missing from her life.

"I said I was sorry," she told him.

Now, he looked hurt. She had closed a door between them, she saw that. He'd been trying to explain how he felt, and she'd stopped him.

"Go upstairs and change into dry clothes," he said. "I'll fix us some pancakes and hot cocoa."

Pancakes and cocoa were about the only foods her father knew how to cook. He was okay with grilled cheese sandwiches, too. It was a good thing they were favorites of hers, because he didn't seem likely to learn how to make anything else.

Grandma Jane had filled in the gaps for all the things Taylor's father couldn't do. Or wouldn't do. Sometimes, Taylor thought it was more wouldn't than couldn't. He just *didn't* do the things a parent was supposed to do with their child. For one thing, he didn't talk to her very much. Their house was mostly silent. Maybe that was why she had turned to Grandma Jane for friendship. For love.

Upstairs in her room, Taylor changed into warm, dry clothes. She picked up the book from where she'd laid it on the bed. Its cover was dry. The rain hadn't damaged it at all. That was good. She'd promised Mr. Ambrose to return the book, and didn't want it to be in worse shape when it came back than when she'd received it.

Her feet were warm and toasty in thick, dry socks. She curled up on the covers of the bed, listened to the storm pounding at the outside of the windows, and opened the book. Her father would call her when dinner was ready. Until then, she turned the pages, and began to read.

It had been raining for five days, and off and on for two weeks before that. That afternoon, the rain had stopped and everyone had come out of their houses like moles climbing out of burrows. The earth was saturated with water, soupy with it, the ground squashy to walk upon. On the farm, everyone had been trapped in their houses for so long, the idea of something different to do was irresistible.

"A few hours away from home will do us good," said Abigail Quinton's father. He was trying to convince his wife, Abby's mother, to go with him to the barn dance.

"I don't know," said Abby's mother, sending questioning glances in her daughter's direction. "I don't like the idea of leaving the girls alone. Anything could happen."

"What could happen in a few hours?" asked Abby's father.

The girls in question were the Quintons' daughter, eleven-year-old Abby, and her best friend, Emma Norris. Mr. and Mrs. Norris planned to meet the Quintons at their house, leave Emma with Abby, and the two couples drive on to the barn dance together.

When her mom left the room for a couple of minutes, Abby's dad asked, "You and

Emma do want to stay here by yourselves, don't you?"

"Yes," Abby answered in a hushed, conspiratorial voice.

Her mother came back into the room, and Abby's father said, "You're being a mother hen, Laura. Every living thing needs a little freedom. The girls will be fine. It'll be an adventure for them to be by themselves for a while."

Eventually, he wore her mother down with his persuasive words, just as Abby had known he would. Her father was the most persuasive man she'd ever met. She couldn't imagine anyone ever saying no to him for anything. He had a smile that would crack a grin on the face of a rock, and the merriest eyes of anyone she'd ever seen. He was handsome, too: tall, lean, sandy-haired, not a redhead like Abby.

Abby's red hair and pale skin that burned in the sun were from her grandmother on her mother's side of the family. Her grandmother had died two years before Abby was born, but the genes for red hair had outlasted her. She had her grandmother's hair, but she also had her father's green eyes. Her eyes were the one feature Abby liked about her face. They were just like his, green as reedy ponds.

She loved her mother—no one was as tenderhearted, loving, and kind as her mother—but she idealized her father. To Abby, there was no one on earth to match her dad.

She couldn't wait until Emma got to their house. The night would be an adventure, like her dad had said. She sat by the window and watched the road, thinking about what she and Emma would do after their parents left for the dance.

Ghost stories! They'd sit in Abby's room, turn out the lights, and tell each other scary ghost stories.

Beyond the pane of glass, a wind rose in the trees outside, blowing the branches into weird shapes, like narrow arms reaching for her. Gray rain clouds scudded over the white smile of the slivered moon.

Hurry. Abby sent out her message to Emma on a thought, anxious for the night's excitement to begin. The fingerling branches waved in the wind, and a feeling of anticipation was in the air.

Tonight, something *special* was going to happen.

Dinner was mushy pancakes, burnt bacon, and a glass of milk. Not bad. Taylor actually preferred her bacon a little burned. She guessed it was from eating it that way all the time. Anything less seemed under-cooked.

"Did you finish your homework?"

"I don't have any."

"Don't have any? What's the matter with schools these days?"

"I'm ahead on my homework," she explained. "It's reading."

"Oh."

Their conversations were usually about school. It's what her father asked, what she answered. He never asked how she was feeling. She never tried to tell him. They were almost strangers, living in the same house, but barely knowing anything about each other.

It hadn't been like that with Grandma Jane. With her, Taylor had talked about everything. They used to go on long walks together. They'd sit in the park and watch the squirrels chase each other up the oak trees. Her grandmother would pull her sketch pads and pencils out of the canvas bag she always carried, and they'd draw pictures and talk.

Remembering made Taylor sad. "Grandma Jane said she was drawing me a special picture."

"She did? When?" asked her dad.

"I don't know, a while before she . . ." She didn't want to say the word, *died.*

He pushed the food around on his plate.

Taylor knew she shouldn't have said anything about it. Her dad never knew what to say to her.

"Maybe it's in her house," he suggested.

"Where?"

"I don't know. Where did she like to draw the most?"

"In her bedroom. The light was better there in the morning."

"That's where I'd look," he said. "If she did the sketch, that's where you might find it."

It was a good idea. There was only one problem. Taylor was afraid of dead people. Her grandmother had died in her sleep, at home, in her own bedroom. If she dared to go into the old wooden house to find the sketch . . . What if she saw her grandmother's ghost?

Chapter Three

That night, as Taylor slipped into her bed and lay her head on the downy pillow, she thought of Mr. Ambrose and the store, the strange and fascinating place of marvelous books and . . . Dreamcatchers.

She closed her eyes, and like the storm clouds fuming over the face of the moon, the images came. The space of her dream was dark, like the night sky. Slowly, the beautiful turquoise and silver beads of the Dreamcatcher shone through, where the cross-points of the Web were laced. The fine threads of the Web seemed spun of gold in the dream, glittering fragments of light against the dark palette of the heavens.

As she watched from below, she saw spiraling dreams drifting through the night, falling from the richness of a seeded sky. The dreams burned as brightly as shooting stars, lights to guide the eyes of sleep.

Taylor tried to see the curved borders of the hoop, the round boundary where the Maker's fingers had sealed the threads of the Dreamcatcher, but she couldn't find any end to it. The entire sky was the circle, and the hoop stretched across the universe to Forever.

That was the place Taylor dreamed of . . . Forever. Was her grandmother there? Was her mother? She wanted to see them again. In that hope, she reached above her, touched the golden threads laced even to the ends of the sky, and began to climb.

She climbed the Dreamcatcher, climbed so high up the glittering rungs of the Web, she could barely see the sloping roof of her house. Her world, and the sadness she'd felt there, were far below. Above, perhaps higher than she could climb, was the place of Forever.

"Grandma!" she cried out. "Are you there? Grandma!"

A sudden movement above her shuddered the spun threads of the Web. Taylor clung tightly. She glanced up. Lowering on a slender thread, its eight legs dancing, was an enormous image of a shimmering gold Spider.

Taylor felt the breath catch in her lungs as the Spider descended on a single fine thread of the Web. It stopped just above her, and she stared into the honeycombed jewels of its eyes. Coppered fear laced over Taylor's heart, sealing in her courage.

The Spider stretched forth one delicate leg, its

straight lines gold-furred and shimmering. The leg
did not grab her, but waited patiently, as if Taylor
should reach forth and take hold of it.

"You want me to come with you?" she asked, still
trembling.

A nod of the Spider's body was her answer.

Impulsively, Taylor let go of the Web. At once,
she fell, spinning out of control and dropping fast to
the sloping rooftops below. Sharp visions of tree
limbs, brick chimneys, and pointed church steeples
rose up at her.

"Help!"

The cry was scarcely past her lips, when she felt
the solid substance of something below her, stopping her fall. In the first instant, she was only grateful not to have struck the ground. In the next
second, she realized she rested on the back of the
Spider.

A sudden lurch nearly made Taylor fall again. She
clung to the golden fur on its back, and felt the
Spider begin to climb the Web. It raced over the
laddered rungs, past the beaded jewels caught in the
threads, past the white smile of the moon, past the
gleam of stars, to the place beyond the boundaries of
the Web . . . where dreams scored the polished darkness like silvered comets over a blackened sky.

From here, Taylor heard the peaceful dreams
whisper and sing. Beautiful images to see with the
eyes of sleep. Nestled on the Spider's back, she
watched. Her fears fell away. She wished she could

climb even higher into the hidden world of the sky, to that place where the dreams were made.

As she watched, a dream moved close to her. In its images, she saw her grandmother's face, smiling in happiness, looking back at her. As the dream drifted past her and away, Taylor heard the words her grandmother said, "I'm with you."

The dream fell from the loom of Forever, and slowly spiraled downward, toward the Dream-catcher, and the place of Taylor's home, below. It was meant for her; she knew it.

"Take me back!" she cried excitedly. "Please, please take me back." She needed to be there when the dream slipped through the golden threads of the Web and fell into her world.

The Spider leapt off the foundation of the Web. Down, down, down it dropped, spinning from a single thread. With the gentlest of bumps, Taylor felt the ground below her feet. Felt herself slip back into that well-remembered place of home, and back into the mind and body of the dreamer who slept so soundly in her bed.

Taylor woke to a flash of lightning, and the boom of thunder rattling her windows. She jackknifed up in her bed, and stared into the dark. At first, she was scared by the suddenness of being woken this way. Then, she was disappointed. She had missed her dream of Grandma Jane.

The dream had been coming to her, falling from that place where dreams were born, above the Web. She'd seen her grandma's face, and heard the words, *I'm with you.*

Something hurt so badly inside Taylor, she didn't think she could stand the pain. It wasn't pain like a stomachache or a bad sunburn. It was sadness, a loneliness so deep within her, she didn't begin to know how to make it better. All she knew was that she was alone, and things were never going to be like they were before. Never.

The feeling overwhelmed her. Lost in this steady drum of sorrow, like the ceaseless beat of rain at the window, Taylor switched on the bedside lamp and picked up the book. *Flashflood* was special, she knew that. Somewhere in the printed words of its pages, maybe she could find an end to sadness.

Abby and Emma stood in the doorway and waved goodbye to their parents. Rain started again, slanting on a wind that blew drops against the frame of the house and the girls.

"I'm getting soaked," said Emma.

Abby shut the door and locked it. There was nothing around their farm for miles. No one would bother them, but she still felt safer with a locked front door. She never worried about such things when her parents were home, but now she and Emma were here alone, and the house seemed different.

"Okay, they're gone," said Emma with an attitude of smug overconfidence. "Now what?"

"How about ghost stories?" said Abby.

The look of overconfidence lessened slightly. "Ghost stories? You mean like scary campfire stories?"

"Um-hmm." It was a dare and Abby knew it. If Emma refused, she would be marked forever as the biggest wimp in fifth grade. No way would she let that happen.

"Let's go to the attic and tell them," said Emma.

It was clear that she was upping the dare, but that was okay with Abby. After all, it was her attic. She knew the place a lot better than Emma did. If there was anything spooky in an old, shadowy attic, it was Emma who'd notice it, not Abby.

They started up the stairs, and then Abby remembered something. "It's cold up there. You'd better wear your jacket. I'll get mine, too."

Cold, dark, and alone, a perfect place for telling ghost stories, Abby thought as she raced to her room for her jacket. The storm wasn't a bad touch, either.

She met Emma at the top of the stairs. Together, they climbed the steps to the attic. Abby brought the flashlight. Their farmhouse was pretty old. The attic had never been wired for electricity.

The glare from the flashlight made everything look weird. Even the simplest things seemed scary: a doll's face framed in the circle of light, its eyes and mouth looking kind of creepy in the wavering cast of the flashlight's beam; an old leather jacket and hat hung over a tall standing floor lamp in the corner, as if the lamp were wearing them; and the attic window's wide pane of glass, like a dark eye staring in at them.

Abby spread a blanket on the dusty wooden floor. They sat on it, cross-legged and looking like kids around a campfire. Abby laid the flashlight between them in the center of the blanket. It wasn't a real campfire, but it gave an eerie glow.

"Who wants to go first?"

"You start," said Emma.

"Okay . . ."

Lightning struck something near the house. The flash ripped across the darkened pane of glass, and thunder followed in the next heartbeat.

"That was close," said Emma.

Abby nodded.

Rain hammered the roof, falling in torrents, the storm much heavier than before.

Abby was glad to be inside on a night like this, but she was worried about her parents.

There was a narrow wooden bridge on the road between their farm and the place their parents were going for the barn dance. If the storm was too heavy and the river swelled, the bridge might be washed out. If that happened, either their parents wouldn't make it to the dance, or they'd be stuck on the other side until the river lowered, and wouldn't be able to get back home.

She kept this fear to herself.

"You think we're okay?" asked Emma.

"Sure, 'course we are."

Maybe they were and maybe they weren't, but she wasn't about to act like she was scared, not in front of Emma. "You want to hear the story, or not?"

"I guess so," said Emma, sounding less than enthusiastic, and staring at the window.

"Hey, if you'd rather go downstairs and watch TV . . ."

"No, I want to hear a ghost story," Emma insisted. "Really."

Great, thought Abby. She'd been hoping Emma would chicken out. It was getting too creepy in this attic. The storm seemed louder here, more threatening.

"Okay," said Abby. She picked up the flashlight and held it in her hands, aiming the beam straight up at her face.

"Eewww, that looks weird," said Emma.

"Yeah, I know." She'd seen it in a movie. The storm was like a special effect, and the flashlight helped set the mood.

"One night," Abby began, "in the middle of a terrible storm, water began pouring in a wide stream down the face of the mountain, down to a little town in the foothills below. There was so much water, the ground of the foothills began to slip and move. The rain puddles became streams, and the streams became a river with no banks to hold them. The river raced over the land, moving toward the cemetery at the edge of town."

"Does it have to be a cemetery?" said Emma.

"Yes. Do you want to hear the story, or don't you?"

"Okay, but I don't like to think about being in a cemetery."

"Don't worry," said Abby, "the cemetery's not going to be there for long."

"Eewww," said Emma again, then leaned forward, tucked her chin into the cup of her hands, rested her elbows on her bent knees, and listened.

Outside the isolated farmhouse, rain beat

at the already saturated ground. Abby concentrated so much on the details of the
story, she barely felt the first slip of the
house's foundation on the shifting land.

Taylor hopped out of her warm bed, ran across the
floor in bare feet, and pulled open the window. Cold
air flowed over her, chilling her skin under the thin
nightgown. She made a tent with her hands against
the window screen, leaned her head against the
tented fingers, and peered down.

Rainwater stood in wide puddles on the ground.
Needles of rain danced on the puddles like water
fairies, making moon-silvered lakes that moved and
sparkled in the faint light. A stream of run-off water
flowed down the gutters of the roof, channeling
against the cornerstone wall along the base of the
house. She heard the gushing sound of it, and
thought of the shifting earth beneath the farmhouse
for Abby and Emma.

Sleep and dreams were far away. The storm was
like a dream, changing the real feelings of her normal life. Anything seemed possible. She could easily
imagine the ground beginning to move from the
constant pressure of the water. Believing it possible,
she believed everything else of that night was possible, too.

She *had* seen her grandmother. She *had* journeyed
with the Spider to the edge of the sky's Web. She *had*

seen the dreams falling to Earth below, and the Dreamcatcher stretching its Web across the face of the heavens. Star to star, planet to planet, the Spider's Web—the Dreamcatcher—connected them all.

Chapter Four

Saturday morning was as dark as Friday night. Dawn hid behind a thick layer of rain clouds, like blackened swollen eyes, bruised and weeping. The rain had stopped for a while, but there was nothing cheerful about this day. It was gloomy and cold. It held as much prospect for excitement and adventure as a dark room.

But then . . . a dark room could be interesting, if something were in it.

The idea made Taylor think of the drawing that might be somewhere in Grandma Jane's house. She hadn't been back to the house since her grandmother's death. Her father had been there a couple of times, but he hadn't looked for the drawing.

It might be there. Grandma Jane had said it was a gift, something special. If the drawing was there, Taylor wanted it.

But Grandma Jane had died in the house.

Going into that house alone would be dangerous, exciting. Anything could happen. That's what convinced Taylor to do it. She thought of Abby and Emma. On a day as dull as this one, adventure waited.

She started to write a note to her father, but changed her mind. She'd be back in a few minutes. He probably wouldn't even notice she was gone. If she told him where she was going, he might come to the house looking for her. That would ruin everything. She couldn't explain her feelings, not even to herself, but knew she wanted to be alone in her grandmother's house, as if she might still find something of Grandma Jane there. And she wanted to be the one to find the drawing, all by herself.

It didn't matter if it made a lot of sense; it was how she felt.

She left her house quietly. Her dad wasn't up. He slept late on the weekends, so she'd have an hour or so before he'd even realize she was gone.

Her grandmother's house wasn't far away. She used to walk there every day after school, or if her dad had a late business meeting, she'd go there and spend the night. Grandma Jane's house was like Taylor's second home. Its walls and windows were as familiar to her as those of her own house—a friend.

Now, it was a stranger.

She wished she didn't feel like crying, but seeing

the house made that feeling rise up in her. She felt the sting of tears at the back of her eyes.

I'm not going to cry.

She held back the tears. Her footsteps sounded loud on the stone path to the red porch. Her grandmother's flowers used to bloom along that path, little clumps of Johnny-jump-ups, blue-and-white pansies, and a white froth of sweet alyssum. No flowers bloomed along the garden path now. Probably no one had watered them.

Taylor opened the front door with her key. She'd been eight years old when her grandmother had given her a key of her own.

"You might need it," Grandma Jane had said. "Sometime, I might not be home when you get here," she'd said. "You'll need it to get into the house."

Grandma Jane had *always* been home. That's what was so strange. It was almost as if she'd known this day would happen, that someday Taylor *would* need a key . . . that Grandma Jane wouldn't be here to open the front door.

The house smelled of being closed up for weeks. No fresh air had passed through it from open windows or doors. It didn't smell of newly baked cookies or of hot cocoa. There were no cut flowers from the garden in vases on the tables, and no scent of violets from the perfume her grandmother always wore.

The absence of all these familiar aromas was the

first sign that Grandma Jane wasn't here. Of course, Taylor had known she wouldn't be, but she hadn't realized how different the house would feel without her grandmother in it.

She left the door open for light to see her way around, and maybe because it made her feel safer, too. She could run out an open door if something scared her. Nothing would, she was *sure* nothing would, but she left the door open anyway.

Electricity had been turned off. There was no need for it. No one lived here now. The house had no lights and no heat. The cold wind from the open door blew across the bare floorboards. It followed Taylor into the house like a storm spirit or a wandering ghost.

She moved with a single-minded purpose, up the richly stained mahogany staircase, the feel of the smooth banister rail running beneath her hand. She had come up these same stairs a thousand times before . . . yet now, it was so different.

Her grandmother's bedroom was on the second floor, at the far end of the hallway. Light from the open front door did not follow Taylor this high into the body of the house; there was barely enough light to see her way along the dark wooden tunnel of the hall.

She wished she'd brought a flashlight. The hall seemed longer and darker than she remembered, full of places where something could hide. Someone. She started down the hall with small, cautious steps.

What if her grandmother's ghost was in this house? What if she saw a pale, shadowy figure moving toward her? What should she do? Run?

Absolutely.

Taylor looked about as carefully as anybody could look, but didn't see anything ghostly moving through the hall. She glanced back over her shoulder to make sure nothing was sneaking up behind her. It wasn't her grandmother she feared so much. Her grandmother had always been good to her when she was alive. Taylor didn't think it would be any different, now that Grandma Jane was dead.

What scared her were other things . . . things her grandmother would have protected her from when she was around, but maybe couldn't protect her from now. It was the unknown that made Taylor feel strange and a little afraid to be alone in the silence of this house.

She turned the knob of Grandma Jane's bedroom door and stepped inside.

The room seemed to breathe in when Taylor opened the door. There was a soft rush of sound, like a surprised gasp. For a long moment, Taylor stood in the open doorway, peering into the recesses of darkened corners, and the smooth planes of tabletop, dresser, artist's desk, and neatly made bed. This was where her grandmother had lived, worked, and died.

In that bed, thought Taylor.

The idea almost stopped her at the threshold.

Weren't ghosts supposed to stay in places where they'd died? This place? This room?

Grandma Jane would never hurt me, Taylor decided, and boldly stepped across the threshold.

It *did* feel as if she weren't alone in this room. Memories as alive as singing birds were here, waking dreams that carried her on memory-wings back to the wonderful times she'd spent in this room with her grandmother. She could almost see Grandma Jane sitting in that old wooden rocker. She'd been a large woman, and the rocker wasn't much more than the size for a child.

Taylor closed her eyes and remembered the sound of the rocker moving on the wooden floor . . . the rocker and Grandma Jane softly humming the tune of an old song. Taylor sat in the rocker for a few minutes and listened.

A warmth of peace wrapped itself around Taylor's shoulders, like a hug. Her eyes still closed, she held the magic of that moment in the dark, and believed . . . she wasn't alone.

"I wanted to say goodbye," Taylor said.

The words hurt her heart, touched it like opening a festering wound, letting the soreness inside begin to heal. She felt the love and strength of her grandmother's arms surrounding her as she sat and slowly rocked in the old oak chair.

"I wish you had told me you'd be leaving," she said, not wanting to say the word *dying.* "Everyone knew but me. Why couldn't you tell me?" Tears slid from beneath the closed lids of her eyes and coursed in warm channels down her cheeks, somehow easing the hurt, the sadness.

"I wanted to say how much I loved you," she told her grandmother. "Maybe you didn't know. I wanted to say it. I needed to tell you. I still love you, Grandma Jane," she cried, "and I miss you so much."

In the comfort of the oak rocking chair, in the soothing sound of its rhythm on the wooden floor, Taylor found her place to say goodbye.

It was a while before she remembered that she'd come here to find the sketch. When she did remember, she carefully searched the room. If the drawing was anywhere in the house, it would be here.

She wasn't afraid anymore. Nothing of harm would ever come to her from her grandmother. Only love. She opened every drawer, and searched in the wide cedar-lined closet where her grandmother's clothes still hung like friendly shadows.

The sketch wasn't there, but she found something else, a gift box from a store. It was tied up with a narrow blue ribbon. She carried the box to her grandmother's bed, sat on the quilted bedspread, and pulled the ends of the bow, loosening the ribbon. It fell away in soft folds.

Holding her breath, Taylor lifted the box's lid. Inside were pieces of her life, saved and treasured by a grandmother who had loved her. Taylor's thin fingers brushed over the photographs, school pic-

tures, drawings she had made in kindergarten, letters and postcards she had written from camp. There
were other cards, too: Christmas cards she'd made,
greeting cards she'd sent for holidays, birthdays,
Mother's Day.

Grandma Jane had saved them all.

It was too lonely to look through them and not
feel the loss of someone who she'd loved so much.
She held the narrow blue ribbon in her fingers, as if
she were holding her grandma's hand, lay down on
the quilt-covered bed, and cried herself to sleep.

Chapter Five

A sound intruded, waking Taylor. She opened her eyes to a darkness deeper than the sleeping edges of her dreams. Daylight had fled the house. The windows were glazed with black. Night ruled. And somewhere, from downstairs, she heard the sound again . . . like a footstep on the wooden floor.

As quietly as she could, Taylor reached for the bedside lamp. *Click.* The switch turned, but nothing happened. *Click.* She turned the switch again, then remembered—no electricity.

A door shut. *Someone going out? Or coming in?*

A footstep on the stairs gave her the answer.

She wanted to run. Wanted to jump off the bed, race out of the room, rush down the stairs, and go home. Her father would be home by now. He'd be waiting for her, worrying, thinking she was lost. She wished she could call him to come get her, but the phone was—

A floorboard creaked beneath someone's weight. Taylor knew that floorboard. It was on the landing at the top of the stairs. Then she saw it, a strip of ghostly light beneath the bedroom door.

Fear stepped into her heart with heavy boots, stepped in and stood there, waiting. The doorknob turned. The bedroom door pushed open, and a light so bright that Taylor had to close her eyes, forced its way into the room.

She gasped.

"Who's there?" a man's voice demanded.

Not a ghost.

"Who's in here?" he asked, and the glow from the flashlight shone around the room.

"Dad?" She called his name softly, in a scared little voice. It didn't sound at all like her.

"Taylor?" The beam of the flashlight caught her, huddled on the bed among the spilled pictures and drawings, her forearm over her eyes to protect them from the glare.

"Do you realize," he said loudly, "I thought you were a burglar!"

"Dad, I'm sorry." She heard the crack in her voice, as if she might cry again.

"Hey, kiddo," he said more gently, lowering the flashlight's beam away from her eyes, "what are you doing here? I got a call from one of your grandmother's neighbors. He said the door to her house was open. I thought someone had broken in."

"I came to look for the sketch," she told him, "and I fell asleep."

"The sketch?"

"The one Grandma promised me. I told you. Don't you remember?"

"Oh, the sketch." He acted as though he remembered, but Taylor was pretty sure he didn't. "Well, did you find it?"

"No." The word sounded so final.

"We'll come back another day," said her dad. "I'll help you search the house. Okay?"

He was trying to be nice; she knew that. "The sketch isn't here. It would have been in this room. That's where she did all her drawings."

"I guess the two of you spent a lot of time here," said her dad.

She didn't answer. Tears were too close. She didn't want to cry.

"Could we go home?" she asked.

"Sure," he said. "We'll go home and I'll fix us some dinner. How's that sound?"

She wasn't hungry. "It sounds good." He was her dad and he was trying to be nice. She could try a little, too.

"Good," he said. "Let's get out of here." He turned to leave.

"Wait!" she called to him. "I want to take this box with me, and all the pictures in it."

She picked up the photos, cards, and drawings from the bed. Her dad helped put them back in the box. The blue ribbon was still around her fingers, as if Grandma Jane were still holding her hand.

"Let me carry that," her dad offered, reaching for the box.

"No," Taylor said. "They're my things, mine and hers. I want to hold them myself."

"Sure." He backed off.

She knew she'd put a distance between herself and her dad, like a wall neither of them could climb. It hurt him. She understood that, but couldn't help it. She didn't want him to be part of her memories with her grandmother. Those were hers alone.

These days, her dad wanted to be part of every-thing in her life, but that wasn't fair. He hadn't wanted that before. Why did he want it so much now?

Being a family couldn't just begin like that. It took time to be close to someone. It had taken Taylor's whole life to be as close as she was to Grandma Jane. Sometimes, she felt guilty that she didn't feel that way about her mother. But she didn't remember her mother. Her grandmother had been the only mother Taylor could remember. And now she'd lost her.

Her dad acted as if he could just begin—start now. It didn't work like that.

"Are you ready to go?" he asked.

She looked around the room one last time. The bed, the rocker, the drawing table. "I'm ready," she said.

They left the house and drove home in silence.

* * *

After dinner, which they ate on trays in front of the TV, Taylor felt loneliness creep over her like a heavy blanket. She needed a friend to talk to. It was strange, the first person she thought of was Abby.

She got up and cleared her dishes from the tray. "I guess I'll go upstairs," she said.

"So early?"

"I'm reading a book."

"Right," he replied, as if she'd told him, *I don't want to be here.*

I'm sorry, she thought, but didn't say the words. Instead, she went upstairs to her room, found her place in *Flashflood,* and began to read.

It was the ghost story. The two girls were in the attic, and Abby was telling Emma about a river of rain washing over the cemetery hill. Outside Abby's house, the rain fell in a steady torrent. The ground beneath Abby's house shifted.

Taylor was there in her mind, in that attic with Abby and Emma, and the sound of constant rain beating on the wood shingles of the roof.

Abby leaned against the wall of the attic, her face close to the cool pane of glass in the window. The sound of the heavy rain helped her think of what to say in the ghost story.

Emma edged closer, too. Her long blond hair fell loose over her shoulders, straight as pulled taffy, and almost the same color. Emma's hair was fine and nearly weightless to the touch, not a heavy horse's mane of red hair like Abby's.

Looking at Emma by the faint glow of the flashlight, she seemed frosted and iced with pink and gold. Abby could imagine how she must look in the same light—orange-red and frizzled. Her hair always bunched up into tight curls when the weather was damp. Carrot-topped hair, heavy, thick, and plumped into bedspring curls, she must look like a ragweed blooming next to Emma. If Emma were a flower, she'd be a graceful lily or maybe an iris. Abby would be something people sneezed at.

"Go on with the story," said Emma.

She was so funny, thought Abby, scared, but interested enough to urge Abby to keep telling it. Emma had a lot of nerve to her. Sometimes it was buried deep, but it was always there. That's why Abby liked her so much. Abby's nerve was on the surface, right where people could see it, like her red hair. Emma's was hidden, like a secret, but they were the same types.

"Rain came down so hard that night," said Abby, "it threaded into little branches of a fast-running river. The water branches dug at the ground, easing it away from the edges of the old tombstones on the hill, loosening the sandy earth of the grave plots.''

"This is *so creepy*,'' said Emma, settling closer.

Abby could tell she was loving the story.

"The rainwater washed down the mountain, over the cemetery hill, and right down the main street of town. As the water washed over the ground, it picked up bits of brown earth, clumps and clods, until it ran like a thickening river of shiny mud.''

"Gross,'' said Emma.

Abby's house shuddered again, but she barely noticed it. Her attention was on the story, and trying to get a good scare into Emma.

"Pretty soon, the water was so sludgy with mud and grass, the weight of it dug tunnels in the weakened hillside, pulling out big chunks of land and carrying them downstream, toward town. Rain soaked in and tore the ground loose, dirt, tombstones, and the first coffins . . . prying the boxes right out of the graves.''

"Ohmygosh,'' said Emma, breathing it out like one word. Her pink-and-white face pulled into a serious scowl of concentration. She was hooked into the story like a fish on a line.

Got her, thought Abby.

"As those coffins rolled down the hill," said Abby, "some of them broke open, spilling out the bodies."

"I don't want to hear any more," said Emma.

"What's the matter?" Abby asked innocently.

"I don't want to think about dead bodies. In fact, I don't want to hear any ghost stories at all." She stood to leave the attic. "It's too dark up here. Let's go downstairs and turn on the lights."

Abby felt a little zing of triumph. She'd accomplished her goal of scaring Emma good. The rest of the night would be dull in comparison.

She got up to follow her, but as she stood, she glanced out the window at the rain. What she saw made her scream Emma's name.

"Emma!" she cried. "Flashflood!"

A wall of water over ten feet high, surged over the ground, heading right for their house.

The water would hit before they could run from the house. It would hit with a force strong enough to knock the whole house off its foundation. It was higher than most of the house, even higher than the attic window. In another minute, it would pour into the room where they stood, and drown them.

Abby's strong arms pulled up the window sash. "We've got to make it to the roof," she yelled to Emma. "It's our only chance."

They stood in the frame of the window, grabbing at the wooden shingles of the roof, and scrambled up. The shingles hurt Abby's bare knees, but she kept climbing. The sound of the wall of water rushing at them roared in her ears.

"Hold onto the roof beam!" she yelled to Emma, who was right behind her.

Those were the last words Abby said before the water hit. The impact sounded like a freight train crashing into the walls of the house. It hit so hard, it nearly knocked her off the roof . . . straight into the churning river.

Chapter Six

Abby heard Emma scream when the house broke free and moved with the force of the water. It was a high, thin scream. Terror-filled. Abby felt like screaming, too, but she was concentrating too hard on hanging onto the top ridge of the roof.

Below her, a dark sweep of water rushed by in an angry swell. Whole trees swirled in the deep water, torn from their roots by the same unstoppable force that had knocked the farmhouse off its foundation.

Other things surfaced for an instant in the water, then were pulled down again by the weight of the flood: the wheels of an overturned car, fence posts, a wooden chair looking as if someone could sit on it and float down the swift running river, and the bodies of animals caught in the sudden torrent of the flashflood.

If any living thing fell into that water, Abby thought, it would be crushed by all the debris twisting and turning in the surging river . . . if it didn't drown first.

Where was Emma? She couldn't see her.

Beneath her, Abby felt the walls of the house crumble and break away. Sturdy wooden walls that had held out against storms and wind, were only a frame of sticks against the strength of the flood. Wooden beams cracked, and nails squealed, pried loose from their supports. The roof sank lower, dipping perilously toward the water as the framework of the house fell away beneath it.

"Emma!" Abby shouted, struggling to hold onto the rooftop while leaning over the steeply pitched side to look for her friend. If Emma had fallen into the water . . . No, she couldn't think that. "Emma!" she called again, using all the air in her lungs.

The roof started spinning in the water, caught in a whirlpool of the flood. Abby lay flat against the roof's spine, pressed her face to its ragged surface, and hung on. The spinning nauseated and terrified her, making her so dizzy, she could barely cling to the ridge beam.

"Abby!" a small voice intruded, scraping across Abby's senses like a rock over chalkboard.

"Emma!" she yelled back. It was all she could do.

The spinning was awful. How much longer could she hold on? Heavy objects in the water slammed into the roof. Something very heavy struck, jarring them out of the whirlpool.

Now the flashflood carried the roof at a rushing speed again, bumping and crashing, like a raft going over white-water rapids. When it hit things, it lifted in the water, then crashed down again with terrible force. Each time this happened, Abby feared the roof would break apart.

Ahead, she saw an oak tree, wide and tall, standing directly in the path of the flood. The roof would hit it, she was sure. She couldn't jump, couldn't dive into that churning swell of river. There was nothing to do but hang on with all her strength, and hope that she wouldn't be flung into the dark and desperate water.

"Abby," Emma screamed, "I'm falling!"

She saw Emma now, on one side of the steeply pitched roof, her small fingers gripped around the fragile wooden shingles, her feet only inches from the water. As Abby watched in terror, Emma slipped a few inches. Now her feet dragged in the water.

"Don't let go!" Abby yelled.

"I'm scared." Emma's face showed how awful her fear was. "I'm so scared." She stared up at Abby for help.

"Don't move," Abby warned. "I'm coming to get you."

She gripped the roof ridge as tightly as she could with the fingers of one hand, then leaned over the side, letting herself slide toward Emma. It was terrifying, seeing the floodwater so close to her face. If her fingers slipped from the ridge . . .

"Grab my hand," she shouted to Emma.

She extended her arm as far as she could, trying to reach Emma's outstretched fingers. Her muscles ached with the tremendous effort of holding so tightly to the roof and pulling so hard in the other direction, working to save her friend.

"Don't lose me," Emma cried. There was panic in her eyes. Her hand waved above her frantically, trying to catch Abby's fingers.

"I'm right here," Abby yelled, hoping she could be heard over the roar of the water. "I'm with you."

A little farther . . . that's all it would take. Abby balanced as well as she could on the shingles and edged down the side of the roof another couple of inches. Her hand touched Emma's, and their fingers twined and gripped.

"I've got you," Abby shouted. "Climb up!"

"Don't let go." Emma's fear stared into Abby's eyes, as shining as the dark water. Her long blond hair was damp and scraggly, hanging in twisted clumps like wet ropes over her face. "Don't lose me."

"I won't," promised Abby. "Hurry up, climb!"

Emma struggled, pulling herself over the wooden shingles. Her hand slipped once, and splinters of wood dug under her finger-nails and into the tender underside of her fingers.

Her feet still hung in the water, the weight of the flood pulling at them, trying to draw her in.

"Come on," Abby yelled. "Take your feet out of the water."

"I can't." Emma hung by the strength of Abby's hand and arm, but the water was winning.

Abby's eyes nearly scrunched shut, con-centrating with all her might on holding on to the shingles, and on dragging Emma up the side of the roof. Eyelids nearly shut, but she still saw Emma's face . . . a look of helpless-ness staring up at her.

Abby skinned farther down the roof. She *would* save Emma.

She gripped Emma's wrist and yanked hard, dragging her out of the water. Emma's feet scrabbled onto the shingles, skidding and slipping, but finally finding a toe purchase in the narrow wedges between the wood.

Emma climbed the roof frame, balancing on one injured hand and two soaking wet sneakers, moving up . . . until the front end of the roof-raft hit the oak tree with a terrible force . . . tearing her loose from Abby's grip, and sending her body flying off the roof, into the drowning dark folds of the water.

"Emma!" Abby screamed. But it was too late. Emma was gone.

A knock on Taylor's door shattered the illusion of vivid images. Abby and Emma disappeared, and Taylor was returned abruptly to the safety of her room.

The knock came again. Her father's voice called softly, "Taylor, are you still awake?"

Why now? she thought. It was the most exciting point in the story. She really needed to know what happened. There was something about Abby that reminded her of . . . she couldn't think of exactly who, but it was someone she knew very well. And Emma reminded her a little of herself. No, more than a little. When Emma fell into the floodwater, Taylor had felt her heart jump, as though she had fallen, too.

The door opened slightly. Her dad's face peered around the edge of the door frame. "Oh," he said, seeming surprised. "When you didn't answer, I thought you'd fallen asleep with the light on. I was going to turn it off."

He stepped into the room.

"I was reading," she said. "It was at a good part."

He stepped back immediately. "Don't stop. I'm sorry, I didn't mean to interrupt you."

He was leaving. All she had to do was keep quiet. He would be gone and she could get back to the story, but . . .

"Dad—"

"Hmm?" He turned around.

She saw how relieved he was that she'd called him back. From the expression on his face, she knew he really wanted to talk. A surprising thought came to her. Was it possible that her dad was lonely, too?

"Did you want to talk to me about something?"

"It can wait," he said, "unless you'd like to talk now?"

She closed the book. That was hard to do, especially with Emma in the water, but it convinced him. He stepped back into the room.

"I just wanted to say," he began, as if he'd prepared for this and practiced his speech, "I know how badly it hurts to lose someone you love very much.

Your Grandma Jane was like a mother to you . . ." His voice sounded breathless with emotion. "Especially after losing your mother."

She saw her father's pain for the first time. She'd never recognized it before, because she hadn't known what that pain felt like. When her mother had died, Taylor had been too young to understand what happened, didn't even remember it, but the scar of pain from that loss was still etched on her father's face. She saw it now.

"I wanted to make sure you were okay tonight," he said, "that you weren't feeling too . . ."

"Sad," she filled in the missing word.

"Yes," he agreed, "sad."

There was something in the word, and the way he'd said it, that made her feel like crying.

"You missed my mother a lot, after she died, didn't you?"

At first, she thought he wouldn't answer. When he did, he said, "More than I thought I could stand."

That's how Taylor felt now.

"When your mother died," he said, "I pushed everyone else away from me, people who tried to be close. Everyone. It hurt so much, loving someone, then losing her. I couldn't stand the thought of ever being hurt like that again. I even pushed you away," he admitted, looking straight into Taylor's eyes, "my own daughter. I'm sorry for that."

A lump formed in Taylor's throat, like a pressure she couldn't ease. She barely breathed around it.

Couldn't swallow. The lump got bigger and bigger, until she thought her throat would burst.

"I missed you," she managed to say.

When the words were spoken, the hard, painful lump softened and faded. The pressure relaxed. She breathed easier.

"You did?" He seemed surprised.

"It felt like you were gone, too," she told him. "Like my mother."

"Oh, Taylor." He sat at the end of her bed, as though his legs wouldn't hold him.

Something was happening. She felt the moment of change between them, like the slight breeze from an open door.

"I didn't think you even realized," her father said. "Your grandmother took care of you while I was at work. I never understood. I guess I thought too much about myself."

"It doesn't matter." She tried to shut down the feelings. Shut down the feelings and the hurt would go away. Buried deep.

"It *does* matter," he said. "You matter. I've spent so much time grieving for what I've lost, I've ignored what I have. You, my daughter."

If she let herself care about him, she'd be opening another closed door, one that might lead to sadness and pain, just like it had led to the hurt she'd felt when her grandmother died. What if she let herself care, and then he stopped caring? He'd done it before.

He could turn away. It was scary, more scary than Emma falling into the floodwater. *I feel like I'm falling,* thought Taylor, *into a deep and frightening river.* She had to learn to trust her father, and that was hard.

"I've made some bad mistakes in my life," said her father. "Ignoring you was the worst of them."

She almost said, *I'm okay,* but couldn't speak. The words seemed stuck in her throat. She wasn't okay. She was sad, lonely, and feeling as if *she* were the one who was lost. Like Emma, she thought, swept away by the river.

"Do you think," he said, "we could start again, you and I?"

She couldn't answer.

"I'd like to try," he told her, "if it's not too late. I do love you, Taylor. You're my little girl. I should have said it a long time ago, but it's always been true."

She wished he'd stop. *Don't say any more.* If he said any more, she couldn't keep the door to her heart shut. It would break open like the floodwaters from the broken dam. There would be no going back to the way it was before, once that door was forced open. No going back. *If he just wouldn't say any more.*

"I understand if you can't forgive me." He stood. He'd be leaving in a minute. If she kept quiet, he'd go.

He turned toward the door, walking away.

Another moment. He'd be gone.

"It's all right," he said, stepping through the doorway.

"Dad—"

"Yes?"

She hadn't meant to speak, hadn't meant to call him, but something made her do it. She couldn't put a name to that something right then. Maybe it was the force of light from the open door. *Couldn't shut it now. Never could shut it again.*

"We could both try," she said.

He turned back and faced her. "I'd like that."

"Okay," she said, as if they'd made a pact. She and her dad. That was so strange. She wasn't even sure what kind of a pact it was. But it felt right; that was all she knew for sure.

"Good night," he said. His eyes were shining. When he turned away, she thought she saw the glint of a tear on his cheek. He turned out the light.

"Good night," Taylor said, realizing that something had changed. She had a real father. It was as if he'd been hiding all these years. Now, he was here and part of her life.

The door closed softly. Outside, the rain continued to fall. In Taylor's heart, the storm had ended. For the first time since her grandmother's death, she felt she wasn't alone.

Chapter Seven

Sleep came in calming waves, as though someone were brushing her hair. She felt the gentle strokes over her scalp, if not by a hairbrush, then by the touch of an unseen hand.

A dream waited at the edge of her sleep. She drifted toward it, easing into the deeper layer of her unconscious thoughts, like floating on a bobbing surface. It was quiet. Restful.

Then the floating stilled.

Darkness opened, and within the vision of the dream, Taylor saw the store—Broadmore's Used Books and Antiquities. It was as she remembered it, and yet not that, exactly. She saw the books on the shelves, row upon row. Instead of titles, on the front of every book was a person's name. Each book belonged to someone.

Mr. Ambrose was in the store, not sitting behind the large oak desk, but moving from object to ob-

ject, never touching anything, but standing before
each piece as if cataloging it in his mind. In her
dream, Mr. Ambrose's thoughts were visible. She
saw an image of the silver bowl he stood before rise
to the startling worlds of his mind. The bowl re-
mained on the wooden table, but the image had been
stored.

Taylor noticed the knight's suit of armor standing
near the front door, as if guarding the store. She
remembered wishing she could lift the visor of the
helmet and peek inside. Now, in the safety of the
dream, she risked this.

She stood on a chair to reach the visor, the part of
the silvered helmet that covered the eyes of the long-
ago knight who'd worn this suit of armor. Gingerly,
she hooked the tip of one finger under the metal flap
of the visor, and lifted.

Dark brown eyes stared back at her.

"Oh," she cried, dropping the visor shut with a
loud *clang* and nearly falling from the chair.

"Don't be afraid," said Mr. Ambrose. "That's
Ewan the Protector, a very old Celt, a lesser knight
of the Round Table, in fact."

"But," she sputtered, stepping far away from the
suit of armor, *"he's alive."*

"Alive? Hmm . . . ," Mr. Ambrose speculated.
"No, not exactly. You mustn't worry about him. He
was once a character in a book, and now he's here."

A character, she thought, not real. *But those eyes.*

"Have you come for the Dreamcatcher?" Mr. Ambrose asked.

"I don't know," she said. "Is it for me?"

He didn't answer.

At that moment, two girls came into the shop. They were about Taylor's age, one a tall redhead, the other a smaller blonde. Each girl looked familiar, as if Taylor must know them, but she knew she'd never seen them before.

The girl with the red hair touched the Dreamcatcher. She rose on tiptoe and unhooked the hoop from the nail on which it hung. Taylor felt a sudden twinge of sadness. Would they buy the Dreamcatcher? That would be terrible. She'd known it was meant for her. At least, she'd imagined it would be hers, that it already belonged to her, the same way the books on the shelves already belonged to other people.

The redhead handed the Dreamcatcher to the girl with long blond hair that swept down to her waist. "Here, Taylor," the redhead said to the blonde girl. "This is for you."

Taylor? She'd called the girl Taylor!

"Oh, Jane—thank you," said the blonde girl. "You're my best friend."

They didn't pay for the Dreamcatcher, but walked right out of the store with it, with Mr. Ambrose watching. The knight let them pass, never moving a silvered finger to stop them.

"That was mine," said Taylor.

"It can only be yours if you claim it," said Mr. Ambrose, "and know what you're claiming."

"That girl—the one with bright red hair—she said my name."

Mr. Ambrose nodded. "And why shouldn't she? Didn't you recognize her? Didn't you know your grandmother, Taylor?"

"My grandmother?"

The dream began slipping away. She couldn't hold it, couldn't keep the images from disappearing into the lost worlds of sleep. As much as she tried to bring them back, the thoughts of the dream would not quicken again to life.

She woke before morning, while the earth was still clothed in the pale half-light of predawn. She opened her eyes, remembering the dream.

It was cold in the room, but she got out of bed and padded barefoot to the window. Outside, the ground and trees were frosted with sparkling water-light, jewels of dew glistening on green-leafed branches and damp blades of grass.

She looked out at the breathless quiet, as if searching for something she couldn't name. Slowly, images of the dream came back to her, gently lifting to her senses like the golden sun lifted into the vault of the sky.

One clear thought emerged: The girl with red hair had called her friend Taylor.

On the heels of that thought, another one came flying, as if like a shooting star. The red-haired girl's name was Jane, that's what the friend had called her.

"Grandma Jane," said Taylor.

But how could that be? Those girls were the same age as her, not old like her grandmother. And the blonde girl didn't look much like her. Taylor had short brown hair, and that girl's hair was long, nearly to her waist.

The tall girl's hair had been red, thick as a horse's mane, and bedspring curly. Grandma Jane's hair had been cut short, and it was gray and white. It couldn't have been her . . .

Could it?

There was only one place where she could find the answer. If the Dreamcatcher was still in Broadmore's then the dream had been only that—a dream.

She hurried and dressed, hoping the store would be open this early.

Maybe I should tell Dad where I'm going, she thought. *Probably. He'll worry.* She scribbled a note on a sheet of notebook paper from her school binder, stuck it to her pillow, and rushed out of the room and the house.

She wasn't sure why, but she felt that Mr. Ambrose would have the answers to her questions.

The streets between hers and the main boulevard of town were empty of people at this time of day. She liked that. It was as if the whole city were hers, a place of her own making.

She pedaled her bike fast. Even if the store was closed, she could look in the shop window and see if the Dreamcatcher was still hanging from the hook. *It was meant for me,* she thought again, and pedaled faster.

A pearly band of moonlight stretched from the dawn sky to the street in front of Broadmore's. Taylor stared at this bridge, the colors muted by an over-film of white. She thought she could see rich undertones of gold, silver, and blue. It was beautiful, like a fragment of sky lowered to the waking earth.

She parked her bike before the shop and peered in the storefront window of Broadmore's. Inside, Mr. Ambrose sat at his wide oak desk. Taylor tapped softly on the window and he glanced up, not startled, as if he'd been expecting her.

He motioned toward the door.

She turned the knob and stepped into the shop. The knight's suit of armor was the first thing she saw. *Ewan,* she remembered, again tempted to look inside.

"Have you come for the Dreamcatcher?" Mr. Ambrose asked.

That sounded so familiar. Where had she heard those words before? She didn't really understand any of this, but Mr. Ambrose seemed to know what was happening.

"Is it mine?" she asked.

"It can only be yours if you claim it," he said, "and know what you're claiming."

The hoop of the Dreamcatcher still hung on its nail. She was relieved to see it. The woven threads of yarn crossed and uncrossed in spiderweb patterns, holding the turquoise stone and the single feather which hung from the wooden frame.

"I had such a strange dream," she said.

"You came here searching for a dream," he reminded her.

That was true. She'd nearly forgotten. Her grandmother had told her about Broadmore's, that it was a place to find her dreams, if ever she lost them.

"I dreamed about this store last night," she said, glancing around. "And about you."

"Yes." He didn't seem surprised.

"The book you gave me . . ." she began.

"The book found you," he said.

Suddenly, she was nervous. It sounded silly, asking such a thing. Impossible. It had only been a dream. She shouldn't have come here at all.

"You've been reading the story of Abby and Emma," he said, more as a statement than a question.

She nodded.

"And you dreamed about them last night."

"I did?"

She thought about it. Yes, the tall girl with red hair like a horse's mane that frizzled in the damp, that was Abby from the book. She was the girl in the dream. The other girl exactly fit Emma's description from the book. Her hair was blond and long, hanging to her waist, and she looked as if she were frosted and iced with pink and gold.

"But in my dream, they weren't Abby and Emma."

He said nothing.

"They called themselves Jane and Taylor. Taylor's my name," she said.

He nodded.

"Why did they—"

"Dreams are a different kind of reality," said Mr. Ambrose.

"Dreams aren't true."

"Oh, they're true," he said, "but there are many kinds of truth."

She wished she understood.

"You came for the Dreamcatcher," said Mr. Ambrose.

"Yes." Taylor tried to sort it all out. "My grandmother's name was Jane. In my dream, she gave the Dreamcatcher to the one called . . ."

"You," said Mr. Ambrose.

It was weird how he knew things before she told him. This store was weird, and everything in it—the books, the knight's suit of armor, and all the special things on tables and shelves.

"Is this shop magic?" The question came from her without warning. Immediately, she wished she hadn't asked it.

"Do you mean like you?" asked Mr. Ambrose.

"Me? I'm real."

"Everything in this shop is real to someone," he said.

She glanced around her. She could easily believe the knight's suit of armor was real. "Do people know the things in here are waiting for them?"

"Do you know what will happen tomorrow?" Mr. Ambrose asked.

She shook her head.

"All tomorrows are secret. The things in here are secret, too."

She glanced around, realizing that she was looking at rooms full of tomorrows. This *was* the strangest shop she'd ever been in, and Mr. Ambrose was the strangest man she'd ever met. It was hard to feel comfortable here, she realized, no more than a person could feel comfortable out of place and in tomorrow.

"If the Dreamcatcher's for me," she said, staring at the floor in sudden shyness, "could I have it now?"

"Go and take it off the nail," said Mr. Ambrose. "It's been waiting for you."

She had expected him to get it for her, but he stayed where he was behind the desk. "I'd have to stand on a chair," she said. The nail was high on the wall.

He nodded.

She didn't want to stand on anything in this store. Maybe the chair was meant for somebody, and if she stood on it, the chair might twist or turn, and make her fall. She picked one with a tall ladder back, and carefully moved it close to the wall. She stood on the chair for only a moment, long enough to pluck the Dreamcatcher from its place.

"Do I pay you for it?" she asked.

Mr. Ambrose turned away, as if he hadn't heard.

"Is it all right if I just take it?"

Still, he didn't answer.

"I'm leaving now," she called out loudly, holding the Dreamcatcher in front of her as she walked through the store. "I'm taking it home."

It was as if his ears were stopped with plugs.

She passed the knight by the door, wondering suddenly if he would reach out and grab her for stealing. She could almost feel the metal fingers clamp around her arms.

"Goodbye," she called over her shoulder, as she passed through the door.

She wasn't sure what else to do. Excitement laced itself across her heart, squeezing until she felt a rigid tightness in her chest. She swung her leg over her bike, hooked the Dreamcatcher on the handlebar, and pedaled for home as fast as she could.

All the way home, the feather fluttered in the breeze.

Chapter Eight

In her room at home, Taylor hung the Dream-catcher above her bed from a tiny hook in the ceiling. When she was seven, the hook had held a mobile of stars and planets. She stretched out on her bed, staring up. With the window open, the Dream-catcher twisted and turned in the slight breeze.

The turquoise stone, she thought, was what Earth must look like from far away in space, blue-green and woven into the web of all the planets and stars stretched across the universe. She liked that image, remembering the dream of the Spider, the Weaver of the Web.

A knock sounded at her door.

"Come in," she called.

"I thought I'd see if you were awake," said her father. "Want some breakfast?"

It was Sunday, a slow morning for both of them.

"I'm not very hungry," she said. "Could I stay here and read for a while?"

"Sure." He started to go, then glanced back. "Where'd you get that?" He pointed to the Dreamcatcher.

She had to think fast. "Grandma Jane gave it to me," she said.

She could almost hear Mr. Ambrose's voice. *There are many kinds of truth.*

"Really?" Her dad looked surprised.

Everything in this shop is real to someone.

"It was from Jane to Taylor."

Her dad smiled at her words, as if she'd said something funny. She didn't feel very funny, but he was looking at her as if he'd heard more in the words than what she'd said.

"Jane and Taylor, huh? Your grandmother was a nice woman. I owe her a lot," he said. "She filled in all the love you needed when I was . . ."

"Lost," said Taylor.

"Yes, lost." He looked sad for a minute, then brightened. "I'm not lost anymore. I want you to know that."

"Did you find your dream?" she asked him.

"My dream?"

"Grandma Jane said sometimes people lose their dreams, and so they get lost. That's why she gave me the Dreamcatcher."

He stared at the hoop above Taylor's bed. "That's

right," he said. "It took me a long time, but I did find my dream—in you."

Taylor hadn't realized how much she'd needed her father's love, until she felt his loss of it. That surprised her. He had needed to love his child as much as she had needed to receive affection from him. She was his dream.

"Dad," she asked, "do you think Grandma knows how things are now, that I'm okay?" She wanted to believe that so much.

He looked down, not meeting her eyes, as if his words were private, but he would share them with her anyway. "When your mother died," he said, speaking softly, "I asked myself that same question. I wondered if she knew how much I loved and missed her, and if she knew about all the amazing things you were learning to do—crawling, walking, talking."

"Did you find an answer?" asked Taylor.

"I can only tell you my own truth," he said. "I believe she knows how much I still love her, and that she's watching over both of us every day," he said. "That she's part of us right now."

There are many kinds of truth. The words of Mr. Ambrose echoed in Taylor's mind. He was right.

"I'll see you later," her dad said.

"Bye."

In the quiet of her room, Taylor knew she would never feel completely alone again. She had the love of her father, something she'd needed all her life. But now, she'd gained back the love of her grandmother, and something else she hadn't even known she'd missed—the love of her mother, too.

Taylor wanted to finish reading the story. She *really* wanted to know what happened, but the dream worried her. Was it possible that Abby was really Jane and Emma was really Taylor? It didn't make any sense; Taylor and her grandmother had been fifty years apart in age. Still . . .

There were a lot of things about Abby that did remind Taylor of Grandma Jane. Abby was brave. Grandma Jane was always that. Her hair frizzed into curls when the weather was damp. Grandma Jane's hair did that, too. Abby had green eyes like reedy ponds. Dark green eyes were the feature Taylor remembered best about her grandmother.

Just because a thing was possible, didn't make it real.

Everything in this shop is real to someone.

She couldn't get Mr. Ambrose, or what he'd said, out of her mind. He kept popping in, as if her dreams were breaking into her daytime thoughts. He was a very different kind of man, she decided, and *Flashflood* was a very different kind of book.

Sitting beneath the hoop of the Dreamcatcher, Taylor opened the book, turned the pages to where she'd stopped the last time, and began reading.

"Emma!" Abby screamed, but the flash-flood rushed on, pulling her away from her friend. The last she saw was Emma's blond hair slipping beneath the raging depths of the water.

There was nothing she could do. Emma was lost. Abby could only cling to the ridge-line of the roof with one hand and the side shingles with the other. The roof jarred so hard when it hit the tree, she had almost slipped into the flood, too.

Now, she was alone. It was bad enough to be caught in the terror of a flashflood with a friend, but to be alone . . . that was much, much worse. For a moment, courage deserted her. She thought she might slip and fall, too.

But only for a moment. After that, all she could think of was —*I've got to go back, got to find Emma.*

She concentrated on this, holding tightly to the roof as it bumped and floated on the floodwater. It was so dark. She couldn't see the objects rushing by only inches from her face. Once, a tree limb nearly caught her on the cheek, but she turned aside in time to avoid it. She knew animals had been caught by the flood. And maybe people. When she thought of that, she was glad it was so dark. She didn't want to see the bodies.

Hold on, she thought.

The roof scraped over debris in the water. The sounds grew louder and louder, as if the whole roof were breaking apart. The wood frame cracked down the middle, splitting apart and sending Abby spiraling away on the now flat, and much smaller, raft.

When the roof broke, it was as if all the terror of that night broke, too. All of Abby's senses were dulled with exhaustion. At least she could stretch flat on the raft and not have to cling to the side at a perilous angle. She grabbed a few quick breaths, stared into the thick and seamless dark, and waited for the next thing to happen.

It happened sooner than she'd expected. A rough jolt from hitting something, which was submerged beneath the flood, tipped the raft on its side, flinging Abby into the water.

Her arms flailed, trying to grab something, anything, to keep from being pulled down into the depths. Her mouth filled with the taste of murky water. Things she couldn't name touched her bare legs.

Her hand touched a flatness. Purely out of reaction, she grabbed it. Only afterward, did she realize it was the headboard from a bed. Someone had been sleeping in this bed, she imagined. Determined to live, Abby clung to the headboard with both hands, letting the floodwater carry her into the night.

Her feet touched bottom, dragging along the ground, long before the raft came to rest on an earthen shoal. The water was barely wading-deep, with no force left to it.

Stumbling, Abby slogged through the muddy stream to the nearby incline of hilly ground. She stepped out on solid land, crumbling though it was, and climbed the swell of earth until she stood trembling and safe, well above the waning floodwater.

The rain had stopped. Above her, clouds parted, and light from a sprinkle of stars penetrated through the darkness. She stared at the glimmer of those few stars, gaining courage from them, and the strength to go on.

Taylor felt as if she'd been riding the flashflood with Abby, felt the shock of Emma's falling, endured the desperate struggle of clinging to the ridgeline, the terror of the roof breaking in half, and the horrifying plunge into the murky depths when the raft overturned and tipped Abby into the water.

In a strange way, Taylor knew she had *comforted* Abby by reading the book. It was as though they really were together. *If I were in a fix like that,* she thought, *I'd want someone who cared to know about it, even if they only read my story in a book.*

She *did* care. The lives of Abby and Emma, Jane and Taylor, had become entwined. Her dream had pushed them together, as if they were the same people. Now, it was hard to imagine them as anyone else. When she thought of her grandmother, the image her mind drew was Abby's face. When she thought of herself with her grandma, it was as Emma.

"Breakfast!" her dad called up the stairs.

"I'm not hungry," she yelled down, hating to stop reading for any reason. She *had* to know what happened.

"It's not an option," yelled her dad. "The food's already on the plates. The book will keep. The eggs won't."

It was so frustrating, having to trudge downstairs, sit at the kitchen table, and force herself to eat. All she wanted was to read the next chapter. Didn't he understand? Hadn't he ever read something that came *alive* for him?

"Your birthday's in a few days," said her dad. "Any ideas about what you'd like for a present?"

Taylor forked a bite of scrambled eggs into her mouth. It was hot and tasty. She was a lot hungrier than she'd thought.

"I don't know. I guess I could use some new clothes."

Her dad pulled a face at that suggestion. "I haven't ever picked out any clothes for you," he admitted. "I don't even know what sizes you wear."

It was true. Grandma Jane had helped her pick out all of her clothes. Taylor was looking forward to the time when she chose her own clothes, but maybe that time was still a little way off.

"We could go to the stores together," she said. "I could tell you what I like, and you could tell me if you think it looks okay—like a team."

"Sounds good to me," he said, looking greatly relieved at having the problem of her birthday present so neatly solved. "We'll have a party, and work together on planning it, just like you said, a team."

Thinking about her upcoming birthday made Taylor feel sad. She'd never celebrated a birthday without Grandma Jane. It wouldn't be the same without the homemade chocolate cake with boiled icing, or the birthday card her grandmother always painted especially for her.

She didn't want a party. But her dad wanted to give her one. He was trying hard to make it work between them. She couldn't let him down.

She rinsed the breakfast plates and loaded them into the dishwasher. On impulse, she washed the skillet in hot, soapy water, saving her dad the trouble. He usually scrubbed whatever pots and pans they used. Maybe it was time she helped out around the house a little more. She was getting older, another birthday in only a few days.

The party might not be *that* bad. She could invite three or four friends from school. Maybe she could talk her dad into letting it turn into a slumber party.

They could watch videos, eat pizza and birthday cake, and . . . tell ghost stories.

Chilled by the memory of two other girls telling ghost stories, Taylor realized how much her life really was entwined with the story of Abby and Emma.

She sat at the kitchen table, trying to puzzle the pieces together in her mind. It was like the flood, pushing her toward something. She didn't understand where this was leading, but knew there was no way to get off until the journey came to an end. Like Abby, she was in for a bumpy ride.

Chapter Nine

Taylor spent the next hour planning her party, thinking of who she'd invite, what they'd do, and what she'd wear. It was fun imagining a slumber party of her friends camped out in sleeping bags in her living room. Her dad had no idea what he was in for. She'd been to the slumber parties of her friends, and they'd been pretty wild. Pillow fights, ghost stories that lasted until early morning, and bleary-eyed parents after a night of little sleep for anyone.

It sounded great.

She called three of her friends, told them about the party, and talked for another two hours about stuff. She hadn't done that for a while. It was nice just to hang out on the phone with her friends. She hooked her knee over the chair leg, scrunched down, and settled in.

Her dad couldn't believe it when he came back to

the living room after two hours and Taylor was still on the phone. "Are you trying for a record?" he asked, only half-kidding. "Go outside, get some sunlight. It's a beautiful day."

She noticed the sun *was* shining. After all the rain they'd had, it was nice to see a blue sky. Her dad didn't know she'd already been outside once this morning, all the way to town. She wasn't lying to him, exactly . . . just not telling him everything.

The thought came to her, certain and sudden: *That's what Grandma Jane did to me.*

It was the thing Taylor hadn't been able to understand, why her grandmother had never told her she was dying. Everyone else had known, her dad, other relatives, but not Taylor. She'd resented her grandmother for keeping that secret, and for not giving them a chance to say goodbye.

Now, she began to understand. Grandma Jane must have thought it was better that Taylor didn't know, that she wouldn't feel sad so much sooner. It was strange. She couldn't remember her grandmother looking sick the last time she'd seen her—a little tired maybe, but not sick.

They'd had fun, laughing about silly things and drawing. Only Taylor hadn't known it would be the last time she'd ever see her. Grandma Jane must have realized, but had kept it to herself. *For my sake,* thought Taylor. Their last day together had been a gift, more precious than any other. Finally, she saw it that way. The resentment that she'd been carrying ever since her grandmother's death melted away.

She went out into the sunlight, as her father had said, and rode her bike to her grandmother's house. It didn't look scary now, only familiar and friendly, like it always had. She used her key and went inside.

The drapes had been closed for a long time. Taylor opened them, letting in the light. She went around the many rooms of the house, opening windows and feeling fresh air moving through the rooms like the coming of spring to a winter garden.

The garden! She remembered Grandma Jane's vegetable rows at the back of the house. Together, they had sowed the seeds from packets last fall. They had put the empty packets on sticks near each planting, so they would remember where they'd put the seeds.

She went into the backyard, letting the screen door bang. There was no need to look at the packets now. The seeds had sprouted. Before her was a lush garden of spring berries and vegetables.

Taylor noticed the strawberries first, ripe and red. All the rain had been good for them. She plucked one from its stem and ate it right in the garden. If spring could have a taste, it would be like this, sweet, juicy, and full of flavor. The berries were ready for picking and eating. From the kitchen, she found a plastic sack with handles, the kind from the grocery store. If she picked the ripe berries, she could carry them home hooked over the handlebars of her bike. They would be a nice surprise for her dad.

She hoped he liked berries, realizing she didn't know.

While she worked in the garden, picking ripe berries and weeding around the plants, she thought of all the things she didn't know about her father and all the things he didn't know about her. They had a lot to learn about each other. They were getting a late start at being a family . . . but there was time.

The sun shone on her back as she worked, holding her in its embrace like the warm hug of a friend. Along the wooden posts she and Grandma Jane had stuck into the ground last fall, were tall vines of pea pods stretching their wispy fingers over the string trellis tied between the posts.

The long pods were fat and bulging with round, delicious baby peas. She ran her thumbnail along one, opening it. Inside were five small green baby peas, nestled in their cocoon-like cradle. She scooped the fresh peas loose from the pod with the back of her thumb, right into her mouth. Of course, they would be better cooked, but even now, crunchy and tasting too green, she thought they were delicious.

In another plastic grocery bag, she collected a harvest of pea pods and two heads of leafy lettuce. She checked on the tomatoes and sweet bell peppers, but they wouldn't be ripe until early summer. The flowering buds on the plants promised there would be many harvest days to come. By the time the red strawberries and green pea pods were gone, the red tomatoes and green bell peppers would be here.

Up until now, the garden had taken care of itself, growing inside the earth until the frost of winter was past. The seeds and ground had done the work, creating plants that pushed their way from the earth and produced something as incredible as a strawberry. Now, it was time for Taylor to help the plants a little, weeding between the rows of the garden and making sure they got enough water.

It was a good thing we had that rain. She should have checked on the garden before. From now on, she'd be in charge of keeping it healthy and growing. In a way, it was as if she were still doing this with her grandmother. They had planted the seeds together. It was their project.

By the time she left the house and headed for home a couple of hours later, she felt a lot better about everything. Life was going along exactly the way it should. Even the gloomy days of rain had brought some good—a garden full of luscious strawberries, leafy lettuce, and sweet spring peas.

Under her covers that night, when the world was dark outside her bedroom window, Taylor turned the pages of *Flashflood* and read about another night and another world of darkness surrounding a child.

Her room sheltered and protected Taylor, but nothing protected Abby. She was alone, lost, frightened, but determined to find Emma and bring her home.

Abby waited on higher ground until the water subsided, until its force was little more than a footbath down a wide stretch of land. The clouds slowly parted, revealing a path where the floodwater had pressed like a weight dragged along the earth.

A cast of moonlight reflected from the wet ground like a dark and shining ribbon. Only when she looked closer could she see the destruction tied to the ribbon's trailing length. Beside the wreckage of homes and farms, were more bodies of animals swept away by the unstoppable waters of the flashflood.

Abby whispered a prayer of thanks for her survival, rested a few minutes to gain her strength, and started back.

Her feet stuck in the mud of the scraped bare path. She tried to walk along the edge of the trail where the land was drier, but slipped often, sinking ankle-deep into the sodden ground.

Her greatest fear was that her foot would touch something buried shallowly in the muddy course. When houses and barns were hit, their timbers had given and burst apart, falling on whatever was trapped inside. There must have been deaths. She saw stark evidence in the too-still bodies of farm livestock—chickens, hogs, even a cat, looking as if he were only sleeping, his body curled beside a stone.

"Emma!" she called into the darkness, as much to give herself the courage of hearing her own voice, as to try to find her friend. A voice meant there was life among all this destruction. Her voice meant she was *here*, not dead.

Amazing things lay in the wreckage left by the floodwater: entire beds, their mattresses still on them, their metal legs stuck in the mud; a kitchen stove, turned on its head upside down in the storm-channeled earth; broken chairs protruding at weird angles, like a ravaged mouth, wet and dark, with sheared-off teeth.

Some things, she tried not to see. Dogs were the hardest. She loved dogs, and many of them had lost their lives in the flood. Other things, she stared at in amazement. It seemed impossible, but a whole room stood before her, its three walls intact. It was all that was left of someone's house. She wondered about the people who had lived in it.

Would she see them along the flood path, too?

It was scary, being out here by herself. She'd never been all alone at night, or wandered far from home. The dark, hidden world of night that looked so threatening from inside a bright, warm house was now all around her. She'd been carried into it, and had to find her way back.

To what?

Abby's house was gone, she'd felt it crumble and break into pieces beneath the terrible strength of the flood. The farm would be gone, too. What about her parents? Were they . . . ?

No. She wouldn't believe that, not until—

Something *moved* beneath her foot.

Abby stumbled back from the spot where she'd stood, staring hard at the thick mud ahead of her. The ground bulged and moved again. It curved toward her.

She wanted to run, yell and run away from here as fast as she could. But what if something alive was in there? What if it was a person? *Emma?*

She dropped to her hands and knees in the mud, and dug through the ooze with searching fingers. "Emma!" she cried, digging frantically. "Don't die," she begged. "Please, don't die."

She felt something solid. It gave a little when she touched it, like a body. Her fingers pulled at thick hair coated with mud. "Emma," she cried again.

The mud held so tight. As fast as Abby dug, and as hard as she pulled, it pulled harder, testing her strength. She clamored to her feet, stood calf-deep in the sludge, put all the muscles of her back into it, and pulled the body from the muddy grave.

She pulled hard. It gave a little. A little more. With a *pop* of released air, the body came free. The sudden weight of it in her arms knocked Abby over, making her fall flat on her back, the mud-covered body on top of her.

It wasn't Emma, but a dog.

Abby gained her balance, and carried the struggling creature to drier ground. "Hold still," she pleaded with it. She wiped and wiped at the mud plastered to its head and body. She laid it on the ground. Weakly, the dog lifted its head. Two cracks like muddy seams opened, and golden-brown eyes stared at her.

"Oh," said Abby. It was all she could think to say. *Oh* for the wonder of it. *Oh* for the beauty of the eyes of a living animal. And *Oh* for the way her heart felt when she saw them.

The dog opened its mouth and breathed.

Abby stayed beside it, letting the exhausted animal rest, as she tried to soothe its fears with gentle strokes of her hand. For a long while, she felt the muscles trembling beneath her palm, and heard how it whined when she took her hand away.

"You're scared, huh?" That wasn't a very bright thing to say. Anything living would have been scared of this flood. "Me, too," she said to the dog, trying to make up for the dumb remark.

After a while, Abby knew she'd have to go on. She couldn't stay any longer. Emma was out there somewhere; she had to find her. But the poor dog! She couldn't stand the thought of leaving him.

"I'll come back for you," she promised the golden-brown eyes. "Don't look at me like that. I will come back, really."

The dog whined softly.

Abby tried not to hear the sound. There was nothing else she could do. She couldn't carry the animal. It was too big, the size of a German shepherd or a Labrador retriever. If she tried to carry him, she'd never get more than a few steps. Tears streaming down her face, she turned her back on the animal and walked away.

A sound like flapping birds made Abby turn

around. It wasn't birds at all, but the dog standing on all four legs, flinging the coating of mud from his body in vigorous shakes. Pointed ears emerged, and the long hair and markings of a collie. Most amazing of all, the dog followed her. He walked carefully, picking his way along the drier stretches of ground.

"Good boy!" called Abby, giving the collie a hug. She hoped he would have the strength to follow her the whole way back. She didn't think she could leave him again.

No longer alone, Abby walked along the flood path, searching for Emma. Every hundred feet or so, she stopped and called to her friend, hoping there would be an answer. None came.

The collie shook itself often, as if it could never get off enough mud. Abby could understand. She tried not to imagine what it must have been like for the dog, caught and struggling for breath in a thick trap of mud. She reached over and petted him again, and was rewarded by a lick on her hand.

"You need a name," she said. She was trying to think of one, when the collie suddenly started to bark.

Abby wouldn't have heard the sound at all, she realized, later. She would have kept walking and never heard the faint call coming from several yards away. She would have passed right by.

The dog heard for her.

"What is it?" Abby asked, following as the dog raced ahead, barking and barking.

Abby picked her way through the flood debris carefully. The noise of the barking was so loud, so insistent, it was a long time before she heard anything else. When she finally heard the voice, sounding weak with exhaustion, she recognized it at once.

"Emma!" she shouted. "You're alive. Oh, Emma!"

Chapter Ten

For Taylor, it was especially good that Emma was alive. Emma was meant to be her in the story—at least, that's how she saw them. She'd believed Emma had drowned in the flood. In a way, Taylor thought she knew what that felt like.

For weeks after her grandmother's death, she'd felt overwhelmed by grief and loneliness, the same way Emma was overwhelmed by the flashflood. *I've been drowning, too,* thought Taylor.

But Abby had found Emma. That was wonderful. *If I could only believe Grandma Jane would find me.*

The thought made Taylor cry. She cried quiet tears that made no sound of weeping. No one could hear her sadness. She kept the loud voice of it locked inside.

She put the book away and closed her eyes. Tears slipped from under her lashes, wetting her pillow and her hair. Taylor's tears were her own flood.

Beneath its waters, she struggled to keep from being pulled under by grief.

When sleep finally came, it was clothed in a beautiful dream. Taylor followed a flowing river of moonlight that streamed from her home to the sky, in a bright channel that stretched across Forever. Unafraid, she stepped into the flow. At its center was the Spider's Web. Taylor touched the shimmering threads and began to climb.

Up, up into the vault of sky, beyond the jeweled stars caught in the Web's tangled threads, up to the place where dreams were found by those who'd lost them. Taylor climbed higher still. She had to find it, that place where her dream waited.

"Grandma!" she called into the dark place. There was no one to hear her voice. "Grandma, I'm so alone."

A soft radiance of light slowly bloomed all around her, surrounding Taylor with the hoop of the Dreamcatcher. The light circled and held her at its center, growing brighter and brighter. In the light were all the rich colors of the earth, like the mix of paints on her grandmother's artist's palette.

It was so beautiful in the circle, Taylor didn't want to leave. She wanted to climb higher, to find that place where her grandmother was. In her heart, she knew; if she climbed beyond this place, she would never return to her home, her father, her friends. With trembling courage, she stretched out her hand to move up the Web.

A shudder on the Web made her glance upward. There she saw the Spider, golden in the radiant colors of the light. From the space above, she heard her grandmother's voice. The sound of it trickled down to her, over the threads of the Spider's Web.

"I'm with you still," said her grandmother's voice, flowing over Taylor in its love. "Go back."

At once, the Web tore into scattered threads, and Taylor slipped down the river of moonlight . . . back through the circle of light . . . back through the scattering of stars . . . back beneath the soft down comforter of her bed. Her head touched the pillow and the dream vanished.

Other roads of sleep claimed her. She moved along them, a watcher of dreams, but none were like the first dream of the night. When she woke with the dawn, she remembered her grandmother's words. They comforted her.

It was very early, the morning still a soft pool of light. Taylor stepped out of bed, wrapped the pillowy comforter around her for warmth, and carried the book to the window where the gentle flow of sunlight filtered over the sill. She leaned her back against the wall, framed the book in the golden light, and began to read.

"I thought I'd be all alone out here forever," said Emma. "The flood carried you away. I looked and looked," she cried, "but I couldn't see you anymore."

"You were looking for me?" Abby was surprised. All this time she'd been worrying about finding Emma. She'd never considered that Emma would be worrying about her.

"I couldn't walk," said Emma, "but I kept watching, hoping I'd see you. I thought about you and thought about you," she said. "You must have felt it."

Abby realized she *had* felt Emma's presence, every time she'd wondered about her. "I guess I did," she admitted.

"I'm so glad to see you," said Emma. "I was scared out here all alone. It's so dark. I thought the flood might come again. I've been sitting here thinking . . . what if nobody ever finds me."

Emma's right leg was broken. She couldn't walk on it, especially through the rough muddy ground.

"I found you," said Abby, trying to sound cheerful. She was scared, too. How were they going to get back home? She couldn't leave Emma, but if she stayed with her, would anyone know they were here? It might be days before they were found.

They waited together, Abby, Emma, and the dog, trying to comfort each other. The collie drew close to Emma, as if he felt the girl's suffering and wanted to befriend her.

Abby tried to make Emma more comfortable, but could see there was a lot of pain from the broken leg.

If she didn't do something soon, the leg would get worse. She had to go back, find help, and bring it to Emma.

When Emma finally started whimpering from pain, Abby made up her mind. "I have to go back."

"No, don't leave me."

"I have to," Abby insisted. "Your leg is getting worse. It might be infected. We can't wait any longer for someone to find us. I have to go back alone."

"No," Emma cried. "If you leave, I'll never see you again."

That scared Abby. Why would Emma think such a thing? "Of course you will. I'll hurry as fast as I can, and when I find help, I'll bring them right back here to you. You'll see me in a few hours."

Emma's eyes were terribly fearful, staring at Abby. "What will I do if you don't come back?"

"I will," said Abby. "I promise."

Emma didn't argue. She lowered her head, as if accepting what must be. It was hard to see that, and even harder to leave Emma alone in this place, hurt and helpless. What if the flood came back? What if something hap-

pened to Abby, and no one ever knew Emma
was here?

Abby carried these thoughts like a burden
on her shoulders. She took a couple of steps
away, then stopped, calling to the dog.
"Come on, boy," she said.

The collie lifted his head from Emma's lap,
but didn't follow Abby.

"What's the matter?" Abby asked. "Come
on, we have to go." She whistled softly to
him.

He stood, but didn't come to her. He
looked from Abby to Emma, as if he couldn't
decide what to do. He took a couple of steps
as if he were going to follow Abby, then
stopped again, whined, and looked back at
Emma.

"I think he wants to stay with you."

"Could he?" asked Emma. "I wouldn't be
alone. Just until you come back, could he
stay?"

"He can do whatever he wants," said
Abby in a voice that didn't sound like her at
all. "He's not my dog, anyway."

It was surprising how much the dog's re-
fusal to go with her hurt Abby. Surprising
and unreasonable. Of course he wanted to
stay with Emma—she was hurt. Animals
sensed things. The dog knew Emma needed
him, that's all.

Still, Abby had been the one to save his life. It had been good to have his company as she walked the path of the flood. She'd already seen terrible things. As the sun rose, she knew she'd see even more. It would have given her courage to have the dog beside her.

"Maybe you should take him, after all," said Emma. "You have to walk through the dark all alone."

"No," said Abby. "I don't need him. I'll be fine."

"Take him," Emma cried. "What if something happens to you?"

"Go back!" Abby said to the dog. "You're too much trouble."

The dog didn't move. It whined again.

"Go on. Go back to Emma."

The collie turned and lay down by Emma's side. It licked her hand, as if saying, *Don't you be mad at me, too.*

"Stay here!" Abby told him. She wouldn't let herself see the golden-brown eyes.

"Trouble, stay with me," said Emma. And then called out to Abby, "Don't forget me."

"I'll be there," Abby promised as she walked away. "Close your eyes and pretend I'm with you still. I'll be there."

She hurried away. The sooner she left, the sooner she could bring help back to Emma.

Sitting along that muddy flood channel couldn't be good for someone with a broken leg. How long before the leg became infected? Or the rain started again? Or something else found Emma?

The thought of *something else* scared Abby. She stared into the folds of night, hoping she'd find her way to safety—for both of them.

Taylor let the morning wake her slowly. It was a cool dawn, and the sound of chirping birds filtered through the open window. She listened for a while, really hearing them. Later in the day, they would only be noises, like trucks on the street or airplanes in the sky, and she wouldn't listen. Right now, they were individual birds, and she heard and appreciated each separate chirp.

It's a nice day, she thought.

That surprised her. She hadn't felt that there had been a nice day in . . . how long?

But this *was* a nice day. The sky was like a cap of jaunty blue, a cheerful and pretty color. The air seemed lighter, too, not stifling and still as it had been for so many days, but cooler and weightless, lifting her spirits. The change in the day was incredible.

Or is it only a change in me?

The thought nearly stopped her. Maybe it was. What difference did it make? Whatever the reason, she felt happier today. It was as if she'd turned a corner, after walking for miles down a long and lonely road, and seen a vision of a different land. A vision . . . a dream.

Maybe she had found her dream, the one she'd lost when her grandmother died. Maybe reading the book had given her that. She couldn't explain how she felt or exactly why, but knew it was better than she'd felt for weeks. Whatever the reason, it was good.

Today was a school morning. She didn't mind. In fact, she looked forward to going to class and seeing her friends. She had a lot to tell them about the birthday party—the *slumber* party. They'd have a great time. She hurried and got dressed, making mental lists of what food they'd have for the party, what music, and what she'd wear. It was going to be fun.

And it was.

The day seemed to brighten as it went along. It began with a good breakfast—the bacon crisp and hot, the toast and jelly tasting sweeter than she remembered them ever tasting before—and a conversation at the table with her dad—a real conversation, not just breakfast talk. That was nice. It was as if they'd turned a corner, too, both she and he. As if they were going in the same direction for once.

A lot of great things happened at school. The regular teacher was on leave, and for the next two weeks, they would have a substitute. Any substitute would have been a nice change, but this one was special.

The substitute was funny, young, and full of fabulous stories. The stories she told were so interesting, it was hard to believe they were really school lessons, and that the class was learning about history—dull, boring history. It wasn't dull and boring the way Miss Langston told it.

Halfway through the morning, Taylor began to wonder, was the teacher really that good, or was she simply part of this magical day? Taylor didn't know, and it didn't matter. She let the rest of the day flow over her like soothing water. Let it carry away all the hurt and sadness she'd been holding since her grandmother's death. Like boxes of heavy weights, the sad feelings dropped away.

She knew now what this day was. It wasn't yesterday, with all the memories of things that had happened in the past. And it wasn't tomorrow, with things she couldn't be sure about. It was today, and she would live in it right now, and be happy.

Chapter Eleven

Mr. Ambrose knew the child would return the book soon. The story was almost finished. He was sure of that. He had felt and seen it in the worlds of his mind. And the story of Abby and Emma had done its job; he knew that, too. Or was it the Dreamcatcher?

Mrs. Broadmore always sent exactly what was needed.

He moved around the shop in a restlessness of spirit, unusual for him. *Something missing,* he thought. *What was it?*

He walked to the store's entrance, where the knight's suit of armor stood. The two pensive figures flanked the doorway, the knight and Mr. Ambrose.

The thought lingered—*What was missing?* The similarity of Emma to Taylor was in the story, and of Abby to Jane. Taylor had seen that in the dreams. The flashflood represented the grandmother's death, separating them, and leaving Emma/Taylor alone and hurt. And the Dreamcatcher, that was to awaken Taylor's mind to watch for her dreams.

But *something* was still missing.

He touched the shining metal of the suit of armor, and in an instant, the suit dissolved into a cloud of sparkles and a shimmering of effervescent light. When the cloud disappeared, Mr. Ambrose wore the suit of armor himself, and walked in it around the bookstore.

Clank, went the sound of his footsteps. *Clank, clank, clank.*

He walked the aisles of the shop, sounding his presence among the mute voices of the books and the unseeing eyes of the china figurines on the shelves. He raised the helmet's visor and stared out at the objects, the books, and the quiet room.

"What's missing?" he asked aloud.

The answer seemed to be a secret.

Yes, thought Mr. Ambrose. *That was it, a secret between Grandma Jane and Taylor.* He wasn't part of it. He wasn't needed. Not the shop, not the book, not even Mrs. Broadmore. It was something special, a message, a gift between Grandma Jane and Taylor.

As soon as he thought of it, he knew what the gift would be. Finding the answer made him so happy, he began to dance around the rooms of the shop in metal-ringing high steps and whirls. If someone had passed by the large front window of the store, he or she would have seen a suit of armor dancing in joy between the aisles of books.

When the shop's door opened unexpectedly, Mr. Ambrose stopped dancing and stood absolutely still, except for the small sound of the helmet's visor slipping quietly over his eyes.

"Mr. Ambrose?" came the child's voice, a girl's by the sound of it. "Mr. Ambrose, are you here?"

It was Taylor McKenzie. He recognized her voice. Had she come to return the book? No, it was too soon. He would have known that, would have been warned, like the sense of winter coming in the air, or knowing there would be rain.

The child walked around the shop, fingering the spines of books, touching a crystal bowl on a table, a wooden pipe on a shelf, touching . . . and moving toward the knight's suit of armor, which wasn't in its normal place by the door.

"That's funny," said Taylor. "Why would he move you over here? You were much better by the door, guarding the shop."

Oh, dear, thought Mr. Ambrose. *What will happen if Taylor touches the suit?* Anything *he* touched changed into moondust and vanished into the worlds of his mind. If the child reached out her hand and . . .

"I wonder if anything's inside you," said Taylor, staring at the suit of armor. "I guess now's my chance to find out."

She reached out her hand to lift the visor of the knight's helmet.

"Oh!" said Taylor, as if she'd felt an electric charge pass through her.

It was so strange. For a minute, everything sparkled like crystalline fragments of diamonds before her eyes. A white glow shimmered in the place where the suit of armor had been, and her hand reached into that glow, as if it were a part of the energy there.

She pulled her hand away.

As quickly as it had flashed into light, the image vanished. One instant it was there, the next, it wasn't. Taylor stood before the suit of armor, blinking in wonder.

"Are you . . . magic?" she whispered.

There came no reply.

"Is anybody in there?" she asked, standing on tiptoe and staring into the open visor.

Two startlingly blue eyes flickered closed. The helmet shifted—a nod, a slight movement of pressure in the room—and the visor clanged shut.

"Mr. Amb . . . " Taylor said, then stepped back, unsure. "No, it couldn't be," she whispered, then turned in a rush and left the shop.

For a long, long time, nothing moved in the store. If any little girl had been watching through the front window from the sidewalk, she would have seen nothing strange or magical. She would have seen nothing move at all. And certainly not a heavy suit of armor.

He waited until night, until it was very, very dark.

Only after he was sure that Taylor had gone, did Mr. Ambrose raise the metal visor of the helmet and glance around. No one there. Not a mouse, not a child, not a soul to see him.

In a brilliant flash of light, Mr. Ambrose emerged from the knight's suit of armor, brushed off his jacket, and smoothed back his white hair. Where a moment before the suit of armor had stood straight and tall, now it was gone. There was nothing left of it but the hint of a sparkle in the air.

Mr. Ambrose tucked the suit of armor neatly into one of the many worlds of his mind. It belonged there, he realized. The knight's suit had been for him, not for anyone else—a gift from Mrs. Broadmore.

A knight in shining armor? he thought. *Is that what I am?*

No, only someone who helped people find their dreams.

It was very late when Mr. Ambrose finally left the store. He thought himself outside the shop—it was far safer than touching the door—and stood on the sidewalk, staring until he found the ladder of moonlight.

Slowly, he began to climb the Spider's lacing Web. Higher and higher, above the wheel of stars, Mr. Ambrose followed the path which led him home.

* * *

Taylor woke late in the night. She kept remembering what she'd seen at Broadmore's bookstore, at least, what she *thought* she'd seen. She had waited outside the shop for a long time, peeking in the window, to see if the suit of armor moved. Of course, it hadn't. When it grew dark, she left and went home, feeling foolish for imagining that she'd seen eyes staring at her from beneath the helmet's raised visor. Two very blue eyes.

It was hard to go back to sleep, wondering about that, and wondering about her birthday on Wednesday. Two more days. They'd have the party on Saturday. At first, she hadn't been looking forward to the party at all, but now she thought about it a lot. She wanted to be happy for a while. It had been a long time since she'd let herself feel happy, not since her grandmother had died.

The memory of her grandmother made Taylor pick up the book. It was almost finished, only another chapter. She hadn't wanted to read the ending, as if somehow that would bring an end to her memories of her grandmother, too.

But now, she switched on the bedside lamp, reached for the book and turned the pages. She needed to know what happened to Abby and Emma, and needed to complete their book before she could go on with her own life. In a way, she felt linked to the journey of these best friends. She was part of it, and they needed her to bring the story to its end.

She sighed, whispering, "I don't want to say goodbye to you," before beginning to read the words of the final chapter.

There was nothing Taylor could do to prevent what she knew would be the end of the book. Even if she didn't read the last pages, that would be an ending. She would still be parted from them. There was nothing she could do to stop the end from coming.

Just like there was nothing I could have done to stop Grandma Jane from dying, Taylor realized at last. *And nothing she could have done to prevent it, either.* It happened because her grandmother had reached the ending of her life, like the ending of a story.

Understanding this at last brought Taylor a warmth she felt all through her. It was the warmth of knowing something was true and accepting it. It was the warmth of letting go of someone she'd loved very much, and still keeping her memory a part of her life forever. It was setting herself free from grief and sadness, and opening the door to tomorrows filled with birthdays and happiness.

"All right," she said, turning to the first page of the last chapter in the book. "I'm ready to say goodbye."

Abby walked the path of destruction the flashflood had left. Everywhere were pieces of houses, broken furniture, the jagged frame of a window, even a half-buried car. Abby peered inside to see if anyone was in it. The car's front seats and backseats were covered with mud, but no bodies were inside.

She was grateful for that. It was bad enough to see dead animals along the path of the flood. She thought over and over to herself as she walked along—*Don't let me see a dead body*.

It was hard to know how far away she was from home. It seemed she had been walking for a very long time. Twice, bright-eyed creatures ran out in front of Abby and scared her, a raccoon and a possum. Each time, she froze in her spot, waited, and they went away.

She wondered if her mom and dad were okay. If they were, they'd be looking for her. It would be so good to see her mother's face or to hear her dad's strong voice. Thinking about them made Abby feel like crying, so she made herself stop thinking of anything but the muddy road she was on.

It would have been good company to have the dog with her. *Trouble*, she thought. That's what Emma called him. *Not bad*. He *had* seen a lot of trouble that night; they all had. Abby liked it. Trouble was a name that fit him. She was glad not to call him *dog* anymore. Trouble he'd been, and Trouble he'd be from now on.

Something sounded on the wind . . . something she almost couldn't hear. It was low as the rumble of a storm, but far away. She listened, afraid it might be another flood heading toward her.

The sound grew louder. Not really a roar, more like a sharp noise. Abby scrambled to higher ground, crouching low to the earth and staring into the darkness ahead of her, waiting.

"Abby!"

Afraid to believe she'd really heard it, she barely breathed.

"Abby! Emma!"

Now she was very sure. She had heard the shout. It was a man's voice—her father's. He was somewhere nearby, searching for her.

"Over here!" she yelled, as loud as she could. "Dad," she cried, "I'm here!"

She couldn't see him moving toward her through the dark, but she could hear his voice. It gave her courage. Back and forth, they yelled to each other, until finally she saw the beam of his flashlight.

"Stay where you are," her father yelled. "I'll come to you."

She knew the fearful journey was over for her. She'd been found, and now she would be safe. Every ounce of strength left her at that moment, and she sank to the ground as if the muscles of her legs had melted.

Safe was a beautiful word.

Only when she felt her father's arms lift her from the ground did Abby begin to cry. The tears spilled down her cheeks and would not stop.

"It's all right," her father said over and over. He stroked her hair and held her, repeating the gentle words, "It's all right now."

In the safety of her father's arms, Abby finally believed these words.

Chapter Twelve

"You'd better get ready for school," said her dad. "I thought you'd be ready by now."

Taylor looked at the clock with sleep-bleary eyes. *Seven-thirty.* Her dad was right. She'd be late for class. She'd stayed up so late reading, and fallen asleep with the book in her hands and the light still on, that she'd slept right through the alarm clock's ringing.

"I'll be there in a minute," she called to her dad, then rushed around her bedroom, throwing on school clothes as fast as she could. She dragged a brush through her hair a couple of times, then raced downstairs, not stopping to even wash her face.

"Hold on," said her dad. "I want you to eat something before you dash out of here."

"Can't," she said. "Even if I run to school, I'm going to be late for class."

"I'll drive you," he said.

"But, you've got to get to work by—"

"Don't worry about me. It's okay once in a while. I don't want to think of you at school without any breakfast. Now sit down and eat what I fixed for you."

She sat in her chair. On the table before her was a plate of French toast and a tall glass of milk. It looked delicious.

"I was hungry," she admitted, eating quickly. "Thanks."

"You're welcome."

She hurried, trying not to gulp, but watching the clock. If her dad drove her to school, she'd make it in plenty of time.

"All set?" he asked, standing in the kitchen, his briefcase in his hand.

"Just as soon as I grab my books," she told him.

She left the house in a far different way than she'd thought she would that morning. Instead of running all the way to school, she sat in her father's car, relaxed and well-fed. The day seemed to be starting out all right, after all.

He dropped her off at the front of the school. "I'll see you tonight," he said. "Have a good day. Love you," he said.

She couldn't remember any other day of her life that had started like this. Her dad was acting like a real parent.

"Love you, too," she said, and meant it.

For an instant, Taylor remembered the scene

she'd read early that morning, when Abby had been found by her father and finally felt safe. When she'd read it, she'd been a little jealous of Abby, but now . . . maybe she'd been found, too.

The slumber party for next Saturday was all her friends talked about in school that day, what they'd do, and how much fun it would be. Everyone Taylor had invited said they'd be coming. It sounded like it might turn out to be a good party, after all.

"Your dad's so nice to let you have a slumber party," said Michelle. "My mom would never let me have one. She says they're too wild. You're lucky."

"I guess so," said Taylor, realizing that maybe this was true.

"I can't picture my father putting together a party like that," said Yasmine. "Your dad sounds great."

"Yeah, I guess he is," said Taylor.

She thought about what the other girls had said, and all day Taylor felt as if her father's arms were around her, holding her in a loving hug.

When she got home from school that day, there was a wrapped box on the kitchen table and a card. The card was from her dad. He must have put the present and the card on the table that morning before they'd left the house.

She opened the card and read his words: *I wanted to give my present to you today, before all the excitement of the party. This was your mother's, and is very special to me. I wanted you to have it, because nothing is more special to me than you. Love, Dad.*

Taylor opened the small, paper-wrapped box. Inside was a velvet-covered jewelry case. She lifted the lid. Lying on a bed of cream-colored silk was a beautiful opal necklace. The stone was milky-white, but when she turned it in the light, she saw bright glints of pink, green, and blue. It was full of colors, but they were hidden in the smooth river of the stone.

Her dad came home from work and walked into the house while Taylor was still looking at the stone. "Do you like it?"

"It's beautiful," she said.

"I hoped you'd think that. It's really from both your mother and me."

That made it even better.

"Thank you," she told him.

Wearing the necklace, Taylor felt that she'd come home at last.

That night, when the world was quiet, Taylor knew she would finish the book. It was a lot like saying goodbye to a best friend who was moving away, and she had put it off as long as she could.

Before this night, she had felt too alone to let Abby and Emma go. Now, wearing her mother's necklace, the gift to her from her parents, Taylor knew the time had come to read the end of the story.

It was after midnight, really the first hour of her birthday. She opened the book and began to read, as if the final pages of the story were Abby and Emma's gift to her.

"You have to find Emma. She's hurt," Abby told the searchers.

Emma's parents were part of the rescue team that had found Abby. "If you hadn't come all this way alone, and in the dark," said Emma's father, "we wouldn't know where to look for her, or even know that she's alive. I don't know how to thank you. Whatever you want . . ."

"Find her," said Abby. It was the only thing she wanted.

Abby's father led her to a temporary shelter, carrying his daughter most of the way. Their home was gone, as were the homes of so many other people, washed away by the flashflood.

The waters of the flood had pressed a weight across the face of the land, destroying everything in its path. Everywhere Abby looked was flattened, with nothing standing on the land, not trees, not houses, not barns. There was nothing left of the farms that had stood in this valley for so many years.

It was hard to imagine that her family's house had stood at the center of what was now a rough cut of mud and debris. In spite of all she saw around her, people were weeping with what they had to be grateful for—the lives of their families. Abby's mother and father were weeping, too, for they said they had what was most important to them, their daughter.

Unable to sleep until she was sure her friend was found, Abby sat on the steps of the shelter and waited for the rescue party to return. No amount of persuasion by her parents could move her from this place of watching the road.

Would Emma be all right? Would they find her?

Abby watched and waited, her eyes fighting to drop closed with tiredness. She sat on the steps, determined to wait no matter how long it took, until she knew Emma was safe.

For a moment, her gaze turned away from the road and stared at the dark gash the flood had scoured across the land. In the early morning light, it looked so awful. How had they survived it?

She wanted to think only of Emma, not of what she saw before her in the flood-ravaged land, but of what she hoped she'd see—her friend. Abby closed her eyes for an instant and tried to remember how Emma had looked when they parted.

Her eyelids had barely touched closed . . .

but that was all it took for exhaustion to claim Abby completely. Without realizing she had gone to sleep, she leaned her head against the porch post, breathed a deep sigh, and drifted off to uninterrupted slumber.

Sleep led her to a place of ease and comfort. Her mind and body rested from the sights and sounds of the flashflood's destruction. She didn't see broken remains of houses, furniture, and dead animals scattered over the land. In the gentle world of her dreams, Abby found the strength to face whatever must come.

She woke a long while later to the sound of the dog's barking.

"Trouble!" she called, waking from the soothing country of her dream, and immediately looked for him.

In a moment, the collie raced toward her, his coat still thick with dried mud. He was full of energy, and by the looks of him, happy to see her. His tail wagged energetically. His feet danced with excitement. His bright eyes stared only at her.

"Good boy," she said, hugging him. It was incredible how happy she was to see him. "Oh, Trouble, they found you. Where's Emma?"

Abby searched the faces nearest her. No

one offered any answer to her question. "Emma," she called.

No reply.

"Emma," she called louder, feeling the fear of the flood wash over her again. *Not again. Don't let me lose her again.*

Then Trouble began barking, and ran from Abby to the group of men approaching the area, carrying a makeshift stretcher. The dog circled the men, and Abby knew it had to be Emma on that stretcher.

Abby's heart stilled a beat. She couldn't move, couldn't breathe, couldn't speak. What if Emma were . . . What if they'd found her too late?

From the stretcher, a hand reached out to ruffle the broad band of white at the dog's neck. "Good boy, Trouble," said the wonderfully familiar voice. "Go find Abby."

Abby drew a deep breath and yelled, "Emma!" She ran toward the stretcher . . . ran to where the collie circled the rescue team . . . ran to Emma, her best friend in the world.

Emma looked as worn-out as Abby felt. Her injured leg was wrapped in a blanket cast, held together by someone's belt. Her eyes looked too tired to stay open, and her blond hair hung in limp strands over her shoulders.

"I told them where to find you," said Abby. "It's going to be okay now. You're safe."

Emma nodded. "You promised you wouldn't forget me," she said, "and you didn't."

The rescue team carried Emma away. She needed a doctor's help for her broken leg. She needed rest and time to heal from all the injuries, physical and emotional, caused by this flood. But she would be all right.

The two of them had been through something they would never forget. It was a bond they shared with each other, something no one else could ever completely understand. They had been there for each other, and part of them would always be there for each other, no matter how far apart their lives took them.

The flood and everything else that had happened didn't matter. They were together. Abby knew with absolute certainty, from now on, everything would be okay.

Taylor felt sad tears well up within her at saying goodbye to the characters of the book. She stared at the final words . . . *everything would be okay.*

Maybe it would be, after all.

On the inside of the back cover was a small bookplate which read: PLEASE RETURN TO BROADMORE'S USED BOOKS AND ANTIQUITIES. Return it? She considered that. It would be hard to let the book go, and harder still to stop thinking about Abby and Emma.

The book had been like a magical dream, but it was impossible to hold onto dreams. *In the morning,* she thought sleepily, *I'll take it back.* It would be like giving a present to someone else, returning the book to the store on her birthday. In a strange way, it would be like giving a present to Abby and Emma . . . *taking them home.*

The book slipped from her fingers, onto the soft blankets of the bed, as Taylor drifted gently into sleep.

Chapter Thirteen

"Happy birthday," said her dad, standing at the open doorway of her room.

Taylor woke to a beautiful, sunny morning. Gold light shone through the window curtains in a lacy pattern of cutout diamonds and swirls, decorating the wall and hardwood floor.

"Good morning," she answered drowsily, enjoying the luxury of waking slowly on a Saturday. No rush to get ready for school.

"Breakfast's ready," he said.

"Um-hmm," she murmured.

"Strawberry waffles."

That got her attention. "Homemade waffles? Not frozen?"

"Not frozen."

"Okay!" She climbed right out of bed and followed her dad downstairs.

The kitchen table was set with her mom's best

china. It surprised her to see the place settings, cream-colored plates rimmed in a fancy design of green and gold. Her dad had gone to a lot of trouble to make everything look pretty.

"I thought these dishes were only for special occasions."

"Your birthday counts as special. Besides," he said, "I think we should have a lot more special days, not hold onto things and keep them put away. If we have beautiful dishes, I think we should use them, don't you?"

"I guess so," said Taylor.

To the side of her plate was a small present wrapped in shiny paper and tied with a wide blue bow. "Is this for me?" she asked.

"Who else?"

"But you gave me my present," she said, fingering the necklace at her throat.

"That was from your mother and me," he explained. "This is just from me. I wanted to find something for you myself. I went shopping and . . . well, just open it."

She tried to imagine her dad shopping for her present. A few days ago, the image would have never fit. It would have seemed impossible. Now, she smiled thinking of him searching the stores for her gift.

"That's so nice," she said, feeling very, very happy. "What is it?"

"Open it and see."

She did, carefully untying the pretty bow, and sliding her finger under the strip of tape on the paper so she wouldn't tear the beautiful wrapping. She wanted to save it. He had gone to so much trouble and—

Inside was a card. Only that. Printed on the card were the words: HUMANE SOCIETY ANIMAL SHELTER.

"What's this?" she asked.

"I thought you might like a dog."

"A dog?" She couldn't believe it.

"Not a puppy," he said. "We're not home enough to take care of one, but a grown dog. I thought we could find one at the shelter. In fact, I saw one I think you will love. Of course, we'll pick the one you want, but this collie is—"

"Collie?" She *really* couldn't believe it. "Did you say a collie?"

"That's right," said her dad. "His coat's a little muddy, but with a good bath, he'll—"

Taylor started up from the table.

"Hey," he complained, "what about your waffles?"

She ate them, stuffing huge mouthfuls in at a time.

"Dee-liss-oss," she said, trying to talk while chewing the syrupy waffle. "Really good."

"Okay," he said, laughing. "Go on."

Taylor left the table and ran up the stairs.

"Where are you going in such a hurry?" called her dad.

"Getting dressed," she called back. "We've got to get him."

"Get who?"

"Trouble," Taylor yelled down the stairs. "He's really there. We've got to bring him home."

Later, Trouble got a bath, a red leather collar, a license, and a leash. When he was washed and combed, he was the best-looking dog in the neighborhood, and Taylor was thrilled to have him.

"He's the greatest present you could have ever given me," she told her dad.

"Well, I guess I didn't do too badly at picking something," he said, looking pleased with himself. "I hope this is going to work out," he said, "a dog named Trouble . . ."

"He's perfect," said Taylor. "Trust me."

Her dad nodded, as if he didn't have much choice.

There was nothing in the world that could have taken Trouble away from her, Taylor thought. Not now. They were meant to be together; she knew it.

Trouble seemed to know it, too.

"It's amazing to me how quickly he's taking up with you," said her dad. "It's almost as though he knows you."

She smiled, but didn't explain anything.

"Could I take him for a walk?" she asked.

"Sure," said her dad, "why not."

She ran upstairs and got the book from her bed.

It was time for all of them to find a home: Trouble, Taylor, Abby, and Emma. She dropped the book into her backpack, slipped its straps over her shoulders, and grabbed the dog's leash.

"Come on, Trouble," she called to the collie. "Let's go for a walk."

It was nice, this slower pace, walking through the streets of the neighborhood, heading toward town. On her bike, everything went by in such a rush. Walking, she noticed more. It was good for Trouble to learn his way around the neighborhood, too.

On the way to town, she passed her grandmother's house. It stood vacant and closed. For a minute, she lingered on the sidewalk outside it. There was nothing there for her, anymore. Her grandmother was gone. That time was something she had to give up, to leave behind her.

But there were wonderful things waiting around the next corner. Trouble was the best dog. Her dad was the best, too. And lots of other things would begin, she realized, each in their own time.

"Come on," she said to her birthday gift, "let's take Abby and Emma home."

Together, they walked toward town. Trouble pulled ahead strongly, as if he almost knew the way. When they got to town, he didn't act nervous or scared of all the people and cars, but seemed eager to hurry along the busy boulevard. When he got to Broadmore's, he stopped.

"You're in on this, aren't you?" said Taylor. "If

I could only know what you know," she wished, "but I guess I'm not supposed to, am I?"

Trouble wagged his considerable tail. Now that he was washed and combed, he really was a beautiful dog. His coat was amber-colored, marked with a wide blaze of white on his chest, underside, neck, and legs. His ears were edged in black, and a fine overcoat of black blended with the amber along his back and tail.

"You'd better stay out here," Taylor said, tying his leash to a post near the storefront. "I don't know if dogs are allowed inside."

Trouble made himself comfortable, lying down on the sidewalk as if he were perfectly content to wait there. His narrow face rested on the white points of his paws.

"I'll be right back," she told him, in case he might be worried.

He didn't look the least bit concerned. He closed his eyes, yawned, and rested.

Taylor opened the door to Broadmore's and stepped inside. The knight's suit of armor was gone. She noticed that first. *Ewan,* she thought, remembering her dream of the brown eyes behind the helmet's visor. Mr. Ambrose had said Ewan was a character from a book. She didn't understand how that could be, how a character could be standing in a bookstore. And yet . . . Trouble had been in a book.

She remembered the day she'd been alone in the

bookstore, and recalled the blue eyes she'd seen when she'd lifted the helmet's visor. Eyes like . . .

"Mr. Ambrose," she said, suddenly noticing him behind the desk.

"I've been expecting you, Taylor."

"You have?" She glanced around the shop. "What happened to the knight?"

"He found another home."

"Was he really from a book?" she asked.

"One I read long ago," said Mr. Ambrose. "I've carried his story with me since then," he said, "and always will."

Taylor thought about leaving the store, taking the book with her and—

"You may leave the book here on my desk," Mr. Ambrose said.

She wasn't absolutely sure she wanted to give it back. The characters had become so real to her, like best friends. It was hard to leave them.

"They'll be all right with me," Mr. Ambrose said, as if he understood her thoughts.

She laid the book on the desk, her fingers lingering on the cover, a loving touch in parting.

"The best thing about a wonderful book," said Mr. Ambrose, "is that it makes us care about the world inside the pages, the people we meet, the story that becomes part of our lives. We carry their story inside us always," he said.

"That's how it feels," said Taylor.

"And what is always with us inside," he said, "cannot be taken away."

She nodded, understanding. "Thank you for lending it to me. I'll never forget Abby and Emma."

"No," he said, "I'm sure you never will."

She turned and started toward the door, but stopped when he called to her, "Taylor—"

"Yes?"

"Happy birthday."

How had he . . . ? "Thanks," she said, and hurried out the door.

Trouble stood eagerly when she approached. For a minute, she knelt beside him and ran her fingers through his warm coat. Hugging him helped to erase the sadness of saying goodbye to Abby and Emma.

"We'd better go home," she said, after a couple of minutes. "Come on." She untied Trouble's leash from the post. "Dad will be waiting."

Mr. Ambrose waited until he was very sure the child had gone. With great caring, he reached across the desk, closed his eyes, and touched one finger to the book.

Sparkling moondust rose in swirls from the cover and the pages. The colors of a world swelled and shimmered in the darkened store. A radiance unlike any brightness on earth glittered in the cloud of pearly dust, circling like a halo around Mr. Ambrose's head. Circling . . . circling . . . until at once, the swirl of moondust disappeared inside the shelter-ing worlds of Mr. Ambrose's mind.

When he opened his eyes, the store was as it had been, with nothing out of place, except the book was gone. It had found its home in Taylor, and was forever in the keeping of Mr. Ambrose.

He listened, and in the thoughts of his mind, he heard the happy voices of Abby and Emma.

Chapter Fourteen

Eight girls had been invited. All of them showed up. The party started on Saturday at three. By four-thirty, the house was noisy with the music and laughter. All of Taylor's friends wanted to see the new dog, Trouble. He didn't seem to mind the attention from welcoming pats, and gobbled up the bits of pizza crust the girls snuck under the table to him.

There was a birthday cake decorated with soft pink roses made from sugar icing set over the frothy sweetness of creamy white frosting. It wasn't the same as her grandmother's home-baked chocolate cake, but it was very nice. After a chorus of singing "Happy Birthday," Taylor made a wish, drew a deep breath, and held it for a moment.

It wouldn't be an ordinary birthday wish. It wasn't for something she wanted. Instead, it was a kind of thank you, sent on the wings of her thoughts, to her grandmother. Somehow, if it was possible, Taylor wanted Grandma Jane to know that she was all right now, that she could be happy again, and that she understood that they would never really lose each other. With all that in her heart, she blew out the tall, thin candles—eleven in a row and one for good luck.

The ring of the doorbell startled her.

"Who's that?" asked her dad. "Another guest?"

"No," said Taylor, "all eight are here."

She glanced out the window and saw a brown delivery van parked on the street in front of her house. On the side of the van was the company name—WESTERN FRAMERS.

Her dad opened the front door. A man stood on the porch, holding a large paper-wrapped package. "I have a delivery for Taylor McKenzie."

"For me?" Taylor stepped closer. All the girls at the party stepped closer, too.

"We didn't order anything," said her dad.

Taylor felt a rush of disappointment, a dropping feeling, like suddenly going up in an elevator. It had been exciting, thinking there was a surprise present for her. She tried to step back, but the other girls had crowded too close.

The delivery man checked his information. "The package isn't something you ordered," he said. "It's from a Mrs. Jane—"

"Grandma Jane!" Taylor shouted. How could it possibly . . . but it was really a present from her grandmother!

"I'll sign for it," said her dad. "And thank you."

"What's in it?" asked Taylor's friend Michelle.

"Go ahead, open it," urged Yasmine.

Taylor's hands trembled as she untied the string and slipped it off the package. Stiff, brown paper was folded over the top, hiding what lay inside.

For an instant, she glanced at her father. Had he done this? *No,* he looked as curious as all the others. It really *was* from Grandma Jane. Taylor lifted the edges of the wrapping paper and spread it open, revealing the present inside.

A framed canvas was turned upside down, its back facing Taylor. On the back was written: *To Taylor, from Grandma.* Below that were the words: *Best Friends.*

It had to be the painting Grandma Jane had made for her. She must have sent it to the framer's shop before she died, and left an order to have the framed picture delivered on the first Saturday after Taylor's birthday. She must have known that's when they'd have a party. That meant her grandmother had been thinking of her, even at the end of her life.

"Turn it over," said one of the other girls.

"Let's see," said Yasmine.

"Go on, Taylor. Turn it over," said her dad.

She lifted the picture by its wooden frame, and in one move, turned it over.

"Who are they?" asked Michelle, standing close beside her.

The painted images of two young girls standing

by a riverbank looked back at Taylor. One was tall, with red hair. The other girl was blonde, with a complexion like pink-and-gold frosting.

"Do you know them?" Michelle wanted to know.

Taylor nodded. She knew them. The painting was of Abby and Emma, just as she'd seen them in her dream, and just as she'd imagined them from the descriptions in the book. Painted onto the foreground between the best friends was a collie dog.

It didn't take long before everyone at the party noticed that Trouble was in the picture. Even her dad was amazed.

"It looks just like him," he said.

It is him, thought Taylor.

She didn't understand how it had happened—how her grandmother had known about Abby, Emma, or Trouble—but something of magic, and love, and forever friendship, had brought this gift to her.

"Thank you, Grandma," she said.

In the quiet of Forever, where dreams and love are born, the whispered words lifted and rose far above the boundary of the skies.

Lifted . . . and were heard.

Here's a sneak preview of what's coming in
The Spider's Child Volume 4: Paintball Warrior!

Ever since his parents died when he was three, twelve-year-old Tyler has been shuffled around from relatives' houses to foster homes. Even though the Jamesons, his new adoptive parents, do all they can to make him feel wanted, Tyler still feels like a stranger in his new home . . . especially around Mark, the Jamesons' natural son. Then, while visiting an old shop in town, Tyler finds a book called *Paintball Warrior*. Cameron Mitchell, the story's hero, is a boy his own age who also has trouble fitting in with his family.

But Tyler's real-life problems don't seem to be getting any better. And when Mark tells him to leave if he's so unhappy with them, Tyler decides to get even. He dares Mark to go with him to the dangerous, off-limits Devil's Gate Canyon. It isn't until disaster strikes and Mark's life is in danger that Tyler realizes it's up to him to save his brother—before he loses the only real family he's ever known!

Dear Reader:

There are many other adventures upcoming in future pages of *The Spider's Child.* The world is full of wonder and excitement. If all the stars in the sky were counted, they couldn't match the number of exciting stories possible to the Weaver of the Web.

If you have enjoyed reading this volume of *The Spider's Child,* I would love to hear from you. I'll try to answer each and every letter from my readers. Send your letters to:

> *Jessica Pierce*
> *c/o Kensington Publishing*
> *850 Third Avenue*
> *New York, NY 10022*

Keep reading!

A Web full of good wishes,

Jessica Pierce